MANHUNT

Iron felt his blood turn cold when the eight outlaws from the camp suddenly emerged from a nearby thicket. He could not keep the shock from showing on his face.

Maynard laughed and said, "Talk about fate, Sheriff. While I was supposed to be chasing down the fella that was on foot, I doubled back to the camp. I found out that Mr. Coffey hates your guts because you killed a friend of his in a gunfight. Since he has this hatred burning in him, and since all these boys like money, they've agreed to help me play a game. A game of hunting . . . and you're the prey."

A cold dread came over Will Iron. Maynard was going to turn him loose, then run him down. With his bad knee, he would be terribly handicapped. What kind of chance would he have of surviving with nine men after him?

Maynard broke into his thoughts. "This turned out even better than I planned." He bent and picked up Iron's Colt .45. Jamming it under his belt, he said, "I'll tell you what. I'm gonna give you a real sporting chance. You've got two hours to run before we come after you. *The Police Gazette* said you're real good as the hunter; let's see how good you are as the hunted. . . ."

The Badge Series
Ask your bookseller for the books you have missed

THE BADGE: BOOK 24

★

THE HUNTED

★

Bill Reno

 Created by the producers of
The White Indian, The First Americans,
and **The Holts: An American Dynasty.**

Book Creations Inc., Canaan, NY • *Lyle Kenyon Engel, Founder*

BANTAM BOOKS
NEW YORK • TORONTO • LONDON • SYDNEY • AUCKLAND

THE HUNTED

*A Bantam Domain Book / published by arrangement with
Book Creations Inc.*

Bantam edition / October 1991

*Produced by Book Creations Inc.
Lyle Kenyon Engel, Founder*

DOMAIN *and the portrayal of a boxed "d" are trademarks
of Bantam Books, a division of
Bantam Doubleday Dell Publishing Group, Inc.*

ISBN 0-553-29251-X

Published simultaneously in the United States and Canada

*Bantam Books are published by Bantam Books, a division of Bantam
Doubleday Dell Publishing Group, Inc. Its trademark, consisting of
the words "Bantam Books" and the portrayal of a rooster, is
Registered in U.S. Patent and Trademark Office and in other
countries. Marca Registrada. Bantam Books, 666 Fifth Avenue,
New York, New York 10103.*

PRINTED IN THE UNITED STATES OF AMERICA

OPM   0 9 8 7 6 5 4 3 2 1

THE HUNTED

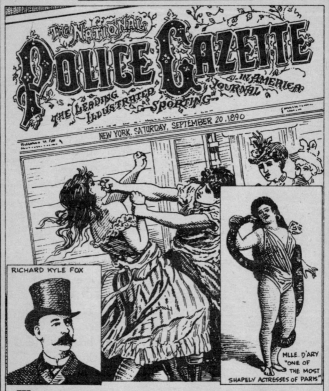

THE NATIONAL POLICE GAZETTE

THE LEADING ILLUSTRATED SPORTING JOURNAL IN AMERICA

NEW YORK, SATURDAY, SEPTEMBER 20, 1890

RICHARD KYLE FOX

MLLE. D'ARY "ONE OF THE MOST SHAPELY ACTRESSES OF PARIS"

When Richard Kyle Fox purchased *The Police Gazette* in 1876, the thirty-year-old publication was a dull, little-read rag featuring criminals and listing the names of army deserters. That all changed when Fox took over, his predilection for scandal and entertainment dictating editorial policy. Sales soared, and Fox prospered. To his credit is the creation of the first sports page, and while his definition of the category included such events as lady wrestling, rat killing, and water drinking, he was largely responsible for making boxing an accepted, legitimate sport.

R. TOELKE '91

© BOOK 1991 CREATIONS INC

BOOK 24: THE HUNTED

Chapter One

Billy Barton's heart was beating painfully fast and the breath was sawing raggedly in his lungs as he ran for his life across the rolling Wyoming prairie. He feared that his nineteenth birthday, celebrated just two months before, would turn out to be his last; he was being hunted by a band of riders from the Circle M Ranch who were fixed in their purpose of ending his life before he reached Casper.

The terror that chilled him to his bones also propelled him on, and he had been running with heretofore unknown stamina through the thick darkness of the moonless night. The darkness was both his enemy and his ally, causing him to stumble often and fall over unseen rough spots and clumps of grass, but also shielding him from the relentless men breathing down his neck. Periodically, he could hear his pursuers behind him, shouting above the rumble of their horses' hooves as they argued about where their prey might be. It was early April, and the night air had a frosty bite to it, but Billy's body was soaked with sweat.

On and on he ran, heading due north. All around him was the bleak stillness of the prairie. There was no one to help him, no one to rescue him from certain death. Keeping low and using the darkness to his advantage, he pressed on toward Casper, knowing now how a helpless rabbit feels when it is hunted by a pack of ravening wolves.

Billy could feel his legs losing strength, and his lungs felt as though they were on fire. He had to rest. Dead ahead he spotted a clump of trees and brush vaguely silhouetted against the starlit sky. Reaching the spot, he stumbled and fell into a ditch beneath the thicket. He bit his lip to keep from crying out against the pain caused by his fall, then quickly crawled to the side of the ditch and hid beneath the overhanging brush, sucking hard for air. His heart was pounding so hard he thought it might burst, and his mouth felt like sandpaper.

While catching his breath, Billy thought back to what had led to this chase, what had happened at dusk some two hours earlier to throw his life into such jeopardy. After a long day's work at the Nelson Hardware Store in Casper, the youth had decided to take a ride and give his horse a good run. He had ridden due south, and as the sun began to set he was some twenty miles from town, nearing the small ranch owned by John and Lucille Tatten. The middle-aged couple had been kind to him ever since he had come to Casper the year before, inviting him to drop by at any time—and if he happened to come at mealtime, he was welcome to put his feet under their table.

Looking at their ranch house, Billy had seen the smoke rising from the kitchen chimney and suddenly felt the emptiness of his stomach. He had shared enough meals with the Tattens to know that whatever Lucille had on the stove would be mighty good. Smiling with anticipation as he approached the house, he had trotted his mount around toward the back. John Tatten had always told him, "Strangers come to the front door; close friends come to the back door."

The smile and the anticipation had immediately faded when, nearing the back of the house, Billy heard the rancher cry out, "No! Please don't shoot us! Please! I beg of you!"

Gunshots had rung out just as Billy rounded the corner. He had pulled rein, staring in shock and disbelief at the sight before him. Wealthy rancher Vic Maynard had shot down the Tattens while five of Maynard's ranch hands looked on impassively.

As the couple fell, sprawling on the ground, all eyes had turned toward the unexpected intruder. Billy's blood had turned to ice as Maynard barked a command at four of his men, ordering them to catch Billy and kill him. The fifth man, Ed Kruse, was to stay with Maynard and help him search for something inside the house.

Wheeling his horse, young Barton had raced toward town as fast as the animal would carry him. But the horse had just run most of the way from Casper and did not have full strength, and after several minutes of chase on the rolling prairie, the Circle M men had begun to gain on Billy. He was nearing a pond when they opened fire. Slugs had ripped into his horse, and when the animal went down, Billy was spilled into the water, beside a jumble of cattails.

Desperate, he had grabbed one of the reeds, torn off a section, and hunkered down beneath the pond's surface. Holding his nose and using the reed as a breathing tube, he had stayed under, praying that when the hunters reached the pond and found no sign of him, they would assume that he had run into the woods of the heavily forested area. By then it was dark enough and the men were far enough back for it to have been possible for Billy to give them the slip.

His ploy had worked. When he finally, cautiously, poked his head out of the water, he had found that the riders were nowhere in sight. After staying where he was a few more minutes to be certain they were not waiting him out, he had climbed out of the pond and started running for Casper.

He had covered better than a mile when he heard thundering hoofbeats behind him. The Circle M men had realized he had tricked them and now were coming after him, knowing he would be heading for town. Giving a quick glance over his shoulder, Billy had barely been able to see them, so he knew they would have a difficult time seeing *him*.

Now, lying low in the ditch beneath the brush, his body aching from being pushed so hard, he could hear the riders trotting their horses around in the darkness, shouting to one another above the wind whipping across the prairie, which shook the brush and bent the trees. More frightened than he had ever been in all his life, young Barton felt as though his skin were crawling, and it took all of his willpower not to scream out.

Billy steeled himself, gritting his teeth. He *had* to make it to Casper and tell Sheriff Will Iron what he had seen. Vic Maynard must not get away with murdering John and Lucille Tatten. Billy told himself that Sheriff Iron was going to be shocked. The wealthy rancher was respected and admired all over Natrona County. The youth knew—as did everyone else in Casper—that Maynard was a widower who had two sons and two daughters living in Nebraska, along with several grandchildren. He seemed the model citizen. No one who knew him would dream that he could kill in cold blood. Billy would not have believed it, either, had he not seen him do it.

Soon the riders moved farther away, their shouting and the sound of hoofbeats growing faint as they scoured the dark land for their prey. Billy did not try to deceive himself. He was fully aware that his chances of evading the four determined men on horseback were extremely thin. Roughly fifteen miles of prairie lay between him and Casper. Sure, there were some small ranches along the way, but the youth knew that if he stopped and asked for help, he would endanger the lives of the ranchers and their families. Billy was certain that the Circle M bunch would kill anyone they had to in order to keep Sheriff Iron from learning who had murdered the Tattens. Billy would only be safe if he was protected by Will Iron's gun.

The wind and the cold night air were chilling him to the bone. His teeth chattered as he scrambled out from under the brush and bounded northward once again, with the Circle M men just barely audible off to the east. Breaking into a run, Billy pushed himself hard for another mile, bending low, darting through patches of brush, and ducking into ditches and shallow ravines. A sharp stitch in his side suddenly stabbed him, but he pushed on, knowing his life depended on his getting to Casper before the riders found him.

But after another half mile or so the pain became excruciating. He had to stop and rest. Diving into a thick patch of brush, he fell to his knees, gripping his side. His throat was raw from breathing the frigid air, he was dizzy, and his head was reeling. Over the sound of his ragged breathing Billy heard his pursuers once again, shouting to one another. They were still some distance behind him, but they were headed his way.

Billy leaned back against a sapling. While he caught his breath and allowed strength to flow back into his trembling legs, the pain in his side eased up. This was a welcome relief. His mouth was so dry that his lips were sticking to his teeth. He rolled his tongue around, but he could not work up any saliva. Then he remembered something his father had once taught him: A pebble would do it. Running his fingers over the ground around him, he located a small stone. He wiped it thoroughly, then stuck it in his mouth. It took only seconds for welcome moisture to flow into his parched mouth.

While working the stone around, Billy told himself he could not let up. He had to stay ahead of his hunters. Giving his respite one more minute, he then forced himself to his feet and began his run once more. He ran in spurts, dropping into low spots and darting behind bushes. But his stamina was about depleted. His lungs were on fire and his legs felt like water.

Finding a ditch lined by thicket, Billy dropped into it, gasping for air. The pain in his side was worse than ever. He found himself longing for his mother, for the solace and protection he had found in her arms whenever he would wake in the middle of the night from a nightmare. His mother's soft voice would lull him back to sleep, her presence security enough. But he had lost that security when he was seven. His mother had died of the fever.

In fact, Billy was an orphan, for his father, too, was dead. He wished his father could have been with him at this moment—his big, strong father who had been a solid source of refuge and with whom Billy had been afraid of nothing. But Frank Barton had died of a heart seizure on Billy's sixteenth birthday.

Suddenly he heard a horse blow, followed by the soft clop of shod hooves, the jangle of bridle metal, and the creak of saddle leather. The Circle M men were almost upon him! Billy clearly heard one of them say, "We've lost him, Carl."

Carl Leedom's voice was as cold as steel as he retorted roughly, "Bah! He's around here somewhere. How far can a skinny kid like that get on foot? Don't you fret none, J. P. We'll catch him afore he reaches Casper. Mark my word—Billy Barton has seen his last sunset."

The words fell like punches on the hunted youth's

ears. Stark terror was like a living thing inside him, gnawing at his guts. As he lay flat on the ground, holding his breath, his heart pounded so hard that he felt sure the killers would hear it. They were no more than twenty or thirty feet away, passing by him as they spoke.

But soon they were out of earshot again. Billy mustered his remaining strength and courage and left the thicket, catching a few faint sounds from the west. Leedom and his friends were combing the area thoroughly. Deciding he dare not take a straight line toward town, the youth ran in a zigzag pattern, going a roundabout way. It would make the journey longer, but it might keep his pursuers from trapping him.

Pausing to rest whenever his body demanded, Billy pushed jaggedly on. Periodically, he heard the Circle M men calling to each other on the prairie and riding their mounts back and forth. When the light of dawn touched the eastern sky, Billy saw a cluster of buildings up ahead. After studying them a few moments, he realized it was Tom Quinn's ranch, which meant he was still a good eight miles from town.

The exhausted young man knew the Quinns well, for the rancher was a regular customer at the hardware store and Billy had helped him and his wife build a chicken coop just a few weeks earlier. If Billy asked for help, they would give it . . . but it could get them and their children killed. Billy would not put them in that kind of danger for his sake.

Looking behind him, he saw the four riders in the distance, coming his way. Heart thumping, he swung his gaze to the horses in the rancher's corral. Rather than endanger the Quinns, Billy decided to take one of their horses and ride for town. Quickly, he dashed for the corral and hopped the pole fence. The horses looked at him disinterestedly. He headed for the barn, assuming he would find a bridle inside. He would not bother to use a saddle; saddling up would only take precious time, and he was adept at riding bareback.

He was almost to the barn door when the rancher's big black mongrel scooted out from under the porch of the house a hundred feet away, growling and making a beeline for the corral. Billy swallowed hard. If the dog set up a ruckus, it would awaken the Quinns—and if Tom got involved, he would face the Circle M riders' guns.

Billy had made friends with Ruff while working on the chicken coop. He only hoped the dog would remember him. As the dog ducked under the bottom rung of the corral fence, young Barton faced him, extending an open hand and saying in a low voice, "Hello, boy. Remember me?"

The dog stopped several feet away and, recognition showing in its eyes, began wagging its bushy tail. Sighing with relief, Billy walked over and patted Ruff's head, then turned back toward the barn. The dog stayed at his heels while he looked around in the semidarkness of the barn's interior for a bridle. He found one and started for the doorway when his eye fell on a large wooden feed bin, its lid smooth and darkened with age. His mind racing, Billy faced the fact that the Circle M men might well catch him; but he could not let Vic Maynard and his men get away with their crimes. Picking up a large nail that lay nearby, he hurriedly scratched a message on the lid:

I witnessed Vic Maynard shoot John and Lucille Tatten. 5 of his men were with him. They know I saw them. 4 are chasing me. I may not get away. Tell Sheriff Iron. Billy Barton

Billy closed the barn door and hurried into the corral

with the bridle, Ruff following. Looking over the half-dozen or so horses, he spied a long-legged chestnut gelding that was no doubt plenty fast. He sidled up to the horse, patted its rump, then slid his hand along its sleek body to its neck. Stroking the animal's neck with his right hand, he slowly eased the bridle over the animal's long face with his left hand. The gelding nickered softly but did not move, and as Billy slipped the bit into its mouth and buckled the chin strap, he could tell the animal had been well trained.

Taking the reins, he led the chestnut out of the corral and closed the gate behind him. Like the horse, the dog was well trained, for Ruff immediately stopped following, sitting down with tongue hanging loosely from jowls. Billy made it onto the horse's back in one leap and guided the gelding farther from the house. Then, ramming his heels into its flanks, he put it into an instant gallop.

Carl Leedom, a big, block-jawed man with sloping, bull-like shoulders and cold eyes, rode just ahead of Dean Dungan, Lou Rippey, and J. P. Ayers, scanning the rolling prairie in the early-morning light. Other than softly waving grass, there was no movement of any kind. Prairie animals had not yet emerged from their holes, and Billy Barton was nowhere in sight.

Where was the kid? Leedom focused on the cluster of buildings off in the distance, the Quinn ranch. Pondering the situation for a moment, he pulled rein, and the others drew alongside. Glancing at them, he said, "Boys, I've been thinkin'. If I was a scared Billy Barton and was attemptin' to get myself to Will Iron in Casper, I'd try to rustle me up some help. Now, everybody in these parts knows that Tom Quinn ain't no pushover, so if you were the kid, and you needed help, and Quinn's place just happened to be on the way to town, what would *you* do?"

"I see what you mean," Ayers agreed. "Seems to me we oughtta check out the Quinn place—and we better get to it pronto. If we don't find that kid and kill him, we may as well not go back to the ranch but just hightail it for South America or some other place far away, because Vic'll have our heads."

"Carl, look!" Rippey suddenly shouted, pointing.

Following their cohort's finger, the pursuers saw a lone rider tearing away from the Quinn place, seemingly pushing the animal beneath him for all it was worth . . . straight toward Casper.

Leedom nodded with satisfaction. "That's gotta be him. Come on, let's get him and be done with it. I need me some sleep."

Billy Barton hunched low on the chestnut's back as he raced toward town. The cold morning air lanced through his clothes, though he was barely aware of it. When he had the animal at top speed, Billy ventured a look behind him. What he saw filled him with new dread. The Circle M men had spotted him and were thundering toward him.

The terrified youth lashed the gelding with the reins, trying to get more speed, but he knew the animal was giving it everything it had. Billy whimpered. There was no way he was going to escape the determined riders. *I know every man has his day to die,* he told himself, *but why did mine have to come so early in life?*

Ten agonizing minutes passed. Hot tears stung Billy's eyes and were immediately whipped away by the force of the wind. Casper was only three or four miles away now. The rooftops of houses and shops were clearly visible on the northern horizon, gleaming in the light of the rising sun. But the men who meant to kill him were drawing closer. He recalled Carl Leedom's words from the night before, that the youth had seen his last sunset. Billy knew he was now seeing his last sunrise as well—and it made him feel sick all over.

The hunters were closing in on their prey. Flashing them a glance, the young man saw them drawing their guns. Suddenly the peaceful morning exploded with gunfire. Bullets hissed all around him. He was doomed. His body seemed weighted down inside with a dreadful heaviness, as though his blood had turned to lead.

Abruptly Billy felt a deep burning pain in his lower back, then a stinging sensation alongside his left ear. He vaguely heard a scream, not even realizing that it was his own, and had a detached impression of falling. The prairie spun in front of his eyes, and then a curtain began to descend, blotting out the view.

Billy Barton pitched off the chestnut, landing in a ditch near the road that led to Casper. The Circle M riders stopped firing and drew rein beside the ditch, lining up alongside it. Lying on his back, the youth tried to get his body to rise, but it refused to do his bidding. The curtain clouding his vision lifted momentarily, and Billy looked up to see his four pursuers staring down at him.

Carl Leedom shook his head slowly. "Too bad you had to come ridin' onto Tatten's place last night, kid. You might've lived to be an old man." He paused, then mumbled to his cronies, "Let's get it over with, boys."

Billy heard the clicking sound of hammers being cocked and looked into the black bores of the revolvers. Wrenching open his mouth, he wailed piteously. But the rising prairie wind carried the sound away as the four guns fired in a succession of roars. Billy Barton jerked and spasmed when the first slugs tore into him, then closed his eyes and slipped into the bottomless black hole of death.

As the smoke cleared, the Circle M riders reloaded their weapons. The grim silence was broken when Leedom shoved his gun into its holster and grunted, "We'd better go take care of Tom Quinn."

Lou Rippey asked, "You really think the kid talked to Tom?"

"He was comin' from Quinn's house, wasn't he?" Leedom countered. He gestured at the horse, which had run off several dozen yards but now stood quietly, placidly munching grass. "And that's his brand on that chestnut."

J. P. Ayers shook his head. "Seems to me if the kid had had time to alert Quinn, Quinn would've been with him. You know, protectin' him so's he could make it to town to spill his guts to Iron."

Leedom rubbed his chin thoughtfully. "True, there's no saddle on the chestnut. Maybe that means the kid just ran onto the Quinn place, grabbed himself a bridle, and slung it on the first horse he could catch. Maybe Quinn don't even know what's happened. I'd rather not kill anyone else if we don't have to." He looked in the direction of the ranch, now a good five miles distant. "Tell you what. Let's ride over and just have a chat with him. Just a neighborly sort of thing. We'll know right off by the look on his face when he sees us if he knows we were partners to the killin' of the Tattens . . . and were chasin' Billy."

Dungan asked, "What about Quinn's horse? Do we just leave him?"

Turning his own mount around, Leedom said, "Sure. Why not? It's bound to find its way home."

The foursome trotted their mounts back down the road toward the Quinn ranch, reaching it just as the sun was coming over the eastern horizon. Tom Quinn was standing on the front porch, a mug in his hand and his big black dog beside him.

The riders were about to turn in to the yard when the rancher raised a hand and waved, smiling.

"No sense botherin' with it, boys," Leedom said quietly. "He wouldn't act like that if he knew we'd been after Billy." As he spoke, Leedom lifted a hand and waved back.

Relieved, the Circle M riders continued on. When they were out of sight of the Quinn ranch, they put their mounts to a gallop, eager to return to Maynard's ranch and report to their boss that Billy Barton was no longer a threat.

Vic Maynard was fifty-six and was showing his years. Though solidly built, his hair was thinning and turning silver, the skin on his face and jaw was beginning to sag, and he had developed a healthy paunch.

The widower was shaving in the bathroom of his huge ranch house, his mind on the men he had sent to kill young Billy Barton. Ed Kruse had reported twenty minutes ago that they had not yet returned; their beds in the bunkhouse were undisturbed. As he stared at his reflection in the mirror, worry scratched at the rancher's mind. Their mission should not have taken all night. They should have had the kid within ten or fifteen minutes. Something must have happened.

Just then heavy footfalls sounded on the back porch, followed by a knock at the door. Quickly wiping the soap from his face with a towel, Maynard tramped down the staircase and through the kitchen, then pulled the door open to find four of his men standing there. Frowning, he grunted, "About time! What took you so long?"

Carl Leedom glanced at the others, then replied, "You're forgettin' it was almost dark when we went after him, boss. He eluded us for the whole night." A smile spread over Leedom's beefy face. "But you don't have to worry about Billy Barton talkin' to Iron . . . or to anyone else."

"Where'd you catch him?" Maynard asked.

" 'Bout three miles outside of town. His body's in a ditch beside the road."

"Nobody saw you?"

"Nope. The job's done, boss, and it was done right."

"Good . . . though I wish it hadn't been necessary— both having to kill young Barton and you having to do the dirty work."

Leedom looked down at his feet for a moment, then asked, "Boss, I know it's none of my business, but I've been wonderin' just why it is that you had to kill the Tattens in the first place."

Maynard stared into the distance. After a lengthy silence, he said, "You boys have more than proven your loyalty to me, so you've sure got a right to know." He shook his head, then explained, "I was a fool kid when I was young, and I got myself in trouble. That was in Oklahoma, where I'm from originally. At any rate, I was sent to prison for robbing banks; did some time in the Oklahoma Territorial Prison. When I was finally released, I went to Nebraska to begin a new life. It was there that I met my late wife, Martha. We married soon after I started courting her and took up ranching. Did well at it, too. Our home was blessed with two sons and two daughters. When they grew up, they all married and settled nearby."

The rancher paused again before continuing. "When Martha died nearly five years ago, I couldn't stand to live in the place we'd called home for so long. It was just too empty without her. So I pulled up stakes and came to Wyoming and bought the Circle M."

Leedom looked at his boss quizzically. "But where do the Tattens come in?"

"I'm getting to that. You see, John Tatten found out

about my criminal past. He has relatives in Oklahoma that he went to visit and—well, somehow my name came up, and one of his kin, a cousin as I recall, knew about my prison record. It seems the cousin was a guard there. The next thing I know, Tatten came to me and threatened to tell my children, who've never known about my record, unless I paid him ten thousand dollars."

Lou Rippey let out a long whistle. "Ten thousand!" he breathed. "That's a fortune!"

"It sure is," Maynard agreed. "But I paid it. It was worth giving him every penny I had to keep my innocent kids from knowing that their father was a convict, a robber. And, besides, I figured that would be the end of it. But Tatten was greedy, egged on by his wife to get even more. When I saw there was going to be no end to the blackmail, I decided to silence them forever." He shook his head slowly, and his eyes glistened with tears. "I just couldn't allow my children or my grandchildren to learn of my past. I'd lose their respect and their love, and I couldn't bear that. They're all I've got." His voice was filled with emotion as he added softly, "And I won't let anything or anyone destroy that."

The ranch hands mumbled that they understood.

Maynard put his hand on Leedom's shoulder. "Yeah, I knew you would. Matter of fact, I chose you four and Ed to go along with me since I know you, too, have stuff in your past that you'd rather not have see the light of day at this point. I know how tough it can be to have a tarnished record, so I was willing to give you a chance and hire you on where a lot of other ranchers weren't." He hesitated before adding, "I hate to ask something else of you. I mean, I know you fellas did what you did out of loyalty to me, and asking you to kill someone was more than I had a right to. But I need you to go back to the Tatten house and take a look around. I want to make certain there's no letter or anything about me that would incriminate me in any way. Me and Ed looked around a bit yesterday, but I just wanted to hightail it out of there. I'd go back and do it myself, but . . ."

"It's okay, Mr. Maynard," Leedom said. "I don't mind. Me and Lou'll go."

"Thanks, boys. It can wait till after you've had yourselves some breakfast and rested up some."

Leedom nodded, and then he and the other cowhands left, heading over to the cookshack.

The rancher returned to the bathroom to finish shaving. Eyeing himself in the mirror, he told his reflection, "Well, you're rid of that blackmailing skunk, and no one will ever know it was you who sent him and his scheming wife to their rewards." He shook his head sadly. "I sure am sorry that that innocent kid had to die as well—but my own kids are far more important to me than Billy Barton could ever be."

Chapter Two

The rising sun streamed in through the kitchen window, warming the room. Vanessa Iron put the bacon-filled skillet onto a back burner. Then, brushing back a stray curl of auburn hair that had fallen in front of her eyes, she called out to her husband, who was still upstairs, "Will, are you about ready? Breakfast is—and so are the children!"

"I'm on my way, Vanessa!" came the response.

A few moments later Natrona County Sheriff Will Iron's footfalls sounded in the hallway, and Vanessa turned to look at him. Though he was now fifty-one, the tall lawman was still rawboned, lean, and tough—in fact, no heavier than he had been twenty years before. Seemingly, his only concession to aging was the fact that his thick hair was now more gray than black. His still-narrow waist sported a securely buckled gun belt, and the thongs from the holster were tied around his muscular right thigh. From the many years she had shared with him Vanessa knew Iron had automatically slipped the Colt .45 Peacemaker from its holster, broken it open, and checked the loads before sliding it back into leather.

Iron and his wife exchanged smiles, her blue eyes and his gray ones meeting in the intimacy that many years of marriage had brought, and then she turned back to the stove and started pouring pancakes into a skillet. Vanessa was ten years her husband's junior but looked even younger than that. No one would argue that she could pass for thirty-five. Her thick, copper-colored hair—which was loosely piled high on her head—was showing only the slightest gray, and she had maintained her trim figure, including a very slender waistline. The tall lawman crossed the large kitchen and planted a loving kiss on the back of her neck. Vanessa smiled with pleasure, leaning against him.

"Mrs. Iron, there isn't another woman on earth who can cook up a breakfast that smells as good as this."

Laughing, Vanessa challenged, "Oh? And what do you base your assessment on, since I daresay you haven't been in the kitchen of every woman in the world?"

Iron gestured theatrically at the two children seated at the kitchen table—his seven-year-old, dark-haired son and his daughter, who at six was a replica of her mother, right down to the copper-colored hair and fair skin. "Why, I have here two renowned authorities on the culinary arts: Miss Amanda Iron and her esteemed brother, Master Joshua Iron. Children, what is your verdict? Is Mommy's cooking the best in all the world?"

Both children giggled, waved their arms, and gleefully shouted their agreement.

The sheriff pulled out his chair at the end of the table and sat down. "There you have it. The matter is settled."

Vanessa laughed as she carried a steaming coffeepot to the table and poured a cup for her husband and one for herself. "I guess you're right. How could I possibly argue with such culinary authorities?"

Amanda looked at her father and asked, "Daddy, what does that mean, anyway? Cul . . . culi . . ."

"Culinary," Iron prompted.

"Yeah. Culimary. What does that mean?"

"Culinary," the lawman corrected. "It refers to cooking."

Joshua snorted and pointed an accusing finger at his sister, who sat across from him. "You didn't even know what an easy word like culinary means!"

Not only was Amanda's hair color the same as her mother's, so were her sky-blue eyes—eyes that could chill you, if she was so inclined. And at that moment she was inclined. Glaring at her brother, she snapped, "Well, if I was in second grade like you, I would have known."

The parents exchanged glances, both of them holding back their laughter.

After a slight pause, the little redhead leaned across the table toward her brother and hissed, "I bet you can't spell it!"

Joshua's cheeks reddened. He lifted his gaze to his father, clearly hoping for support.

But Iron merely stroked his salt-and-pepper mustache and said, "Don't look to me for help, son. One of these days you'll learn never to start an argument with a woman, especially a redhead. You got yourself into this hole . . . now get yourself out."

Joshua scowled at his sister. "You wouldn't know if I spelled it right or not, anyway."

"Mommy and Daddy would," came the tart retort.

Vanessa came to her son's rescue by dropping a steaming pancake on his plate beside two strips of bacon. "There you are, second-grader. Eat."

Amanda was clearly satisfied that she had made her point. She gave her brother a smile of superiority, then lifted her plate for a pancake.

After serving her family, Vanessa filled her own plate, then sat down. All conversation had ended in deference to eating. The redhead looked at her children and thought of the baby who had died of pneumonia in the winter of

1882. Had Will Jr. lived, he would have turned eleven next week. There was a hollow spot in her heart as she wondered what he would have been like. Would he have been tall and slender like his father? Would he have looked as much like Will Sr. as Joshua did?

Forcing the painful memory of her dead child from her mind, Vanessa gazed across the table at her ruggedly handsome husband. She loved his chiseled jaw and the determined jut of his chin. Looking into his gray eyes, she thought of all the outlaws—now lying under the sod—who had also looked into those eyes and had forced Will Iron to draw his gun. His speed and accuracy were unparalleled in these parts—or at least they had been so far. A few men in the past had come close to besting him—some had been fast enough to get off a shot before dying under the lawman's gun—and he carried some scars from their bullets. But now that he was getting on in years, his speed and accuracy had started to slip, if ever so minutely . . . though he would not yet admit it.

When Iron had turned fifty, Vanessa had broached with him the subject of retirement from law enforcement. "No man can outdraw Father Time," she had told him. "Age slows a body's reflexes. It's nothing to be ashamed of. It happens to every man fortunate enough to live into his fifties or beyond."

Iron had not taken the subject of retirement as a lawman easily, and he cooled whenever she brought the subject up. She dreaded talking to him about it again, but her love for him outweighed the dread. *He* was getting older, but there was always a fresh crop of outlaws and young gunfighters who would try to make a name for themselves by challenging and outdrawing the famous sheriff of Natrona County, Wyoming.

Seeing that her husband's cup was almost empty, she got up, took the coffeepot from the stove, and poured him a full cup, receiving his smile of appreciation in return. While standing over him with the coffeepot in hand, she ran her fingers through his coarse hair and said cautiously, "Honey, it won't be long till there isn't a black hair left. I love the gray, though. It's—"

"We're not going to get on the subject of retirement again, are we?" he interrupted.

She chuckled nervously. "You know me like a book, don't you?"

Looking up, he smiled at her and replied, "Well, it's easy. Whenever you start talking about how gray my hair is getting, I know what's coming."

Returning the coffeepot to the stove, Vanessa sat down again and touched her husband's free hand. "Darling, you know I love you with everything in me. I only want what's best for you—and, yes, for the children and me. This is 1891, Will. You're now fifty-one years old. I know you're tired of hearing me say it, but you need to seriously consider stepping aside and letting Jim Stenzel become sheriff."

Iron shifted on the chair and picked up his cup of coffee. Without responding, he blew on the steaming liquid, then took a careful sip.

The children glanced at their mother. Vanessa knew that they understood their father's deep aversion to the thought of stepping aside and turning in his badge. Amanda took a drink of milk, then set the glass down. Wiping away the white ring around her mouth with the back of her hand, she looked at her mother and said, "Mommy, Daddy isn't so old. In fact, I heard Miss Norris, my teacher, say to Mrs. Puckett at the general store yesterday that he's still as good-looking as always."

Arching her eyebrows, Vanessa said, "She said that, did she?" She glanced at her husband, who merely shrugged and looked slightly discomfited.

"Yep. And I agree with her. She also said Daddy's gray hair just makes him look more, um, extinguished."

Iron covered his smile with his hand, and Vanessa struggled to keep from laughing by telling her husband playfully, "Vickie Norris is quite pretty, Sheriff Iron. If little ears were not so big and little mouths were not even bigger, I would tell you how *extinguished* you would truly be if I see her hanging around your office."

The lawman grinned and said, "But, Vanessa, can I help it if others find me ever more handsome and extinguished as I get older?"

The redhead shook her head, grinning, then soberly explained to her daughter, "Amanda, when I speak to Daddy about retiring because of his age, I'm not talking about his looks. I'm talking about his life. If he doesn't turn in his badge and take off his gun soon, one of these days some young gunslick is going to outdraw him because the natural process of aging has slowed him down."

Iron said nothing but rather intently mopped his plate with a piece of bread. It was obvious that the discussion was making him uncomfortable.

Joshua spoke up in his father's defense. "Mommy, no gunslick is ever gonna put Daddy down. He's still the fastest man alive with a gun."

Vanessa's blue eyes assessed her husband, and she smiled, then broke into a hearty laugh. "What have you been doing, Will Iron? Schooling these children when I'm not looking?"

"Of course not, darlin'. These youngsters are just intelligent." Then he added, "Just for the record, I'm still as fast and accurate with my gun as I was twenty-five years ago . . . so maybe I'll consider retiring when I turn sixty."

Vanessa rose from the table, shaking her head, telling herself there was one thing about her husband that age would never modify—his stubbornness. She picked up the coffeepot at the stove, turned, and asked, "More coffee?"

Eyeing her cautiously, Iron queried, "End of discussion about my retirement?"

"For the time being," she conceded.

"Then I'll have another cup," he said, grinning. Suddenly he snapped his fingers. "I just remembered. This is the day that reporter is supposed to arrive from New York."

Giving him a blank look, Vanessa asked, "Reporter? From New York?"

"I guess I forgot to mention it to you. His name is Bernie Tripp. He's with the *Police Gazette*. He sent a letter to the office a month or so ago, asking if he could come to Casper and do a story on me. The chief editor of the *Gazette* seems to think I'm some kind of famous lawman. He's eager for Tripp to come here and do a story on my life and work. I didn't want to be rude to him, so I wrote back and told him to come."

"Why, darling, that's wonderful!" Vanessa exclaimed. "It's about time somebody recognized what you've done and told the world about it!"

Iron eyed his wife with a victorious look that she had seen a thousand times. She knew what was coming even before he said, "Now, sweetie, how would it look if after Tripp plays me up real big in his article, he writes that I'm about to retire?"

"It would look all right to me," she retorted. "You've done more than your share as a lawman. Graves and jails are filled with lawbreakers because of you. Natrona County is a far safer place to live. The whole state of Wyoming is, for that matter. You deserve to be able to step aside now and let a younger man wear the sheriff's badge. I don't care what the readers of that story think. I'd rather see you retire right now and have you by my side for the rest of my life than to stand over your grave." Tears suddenly filled Vanessa's eyes, and she put a hand on her husband's shoulder and said quietly, "I'm pleading with you, Will. Give up your badge before it's too late."

The lawman stood up and took his wife into his arms. Looking deep into her eyes, he said tenderly, "Honey, you worry too much. I'm not going to get myself killed and leave you for some other man to come along and marry. I can still take care of myself."

The redhead looked down and said no more. Iron kissed her cheek, then went out with Joshua to feed the horses and clean out the barn while Vanessa busied herself with washing the breakfast dishes and the skillets.

After completing his chores, the sheriff headed for the office. Arriving there, Will Iron found his deputy busy sweeping out jail cells, all of which were empty at the moment.

Sandy-haired Jim Stenzel was twenty-nine years old, almost as tall as his boss and equally slender. His pale blue eyes and well-trimmed mustache were his most distinctive features, but his ready smile continually lit up his rather plain face. It was just such a smile that now greeted his boss. After returning the greeting, Iron mentioned Bernie Tripp's scheduled arrival on the ten o'clock train, and Stenzel virtually repeated what Vanessa had said: It was about time that the rest of the country knew about Sheriff Will Iron.

The lawmen were catching up on some paperwork when, just before ten o'clock, a middle-aged man burst through the door out of breath and gasped, "Sheriff, trouble's brewin' at the Rusty Lantern!"

Dropping the papers and quickly standing, Iron asked, "What is it?"

"Some gunslick—I don't know his name—is tryin' to

prod young Benny Wilson into a shoot-out. Better get over there fast!"

Iron grabbed his hat off the peg and bolted out the door. As he raced down the street, with Stenzel right beside him, the sheriff was only vaguely aware of the whistle and bell signaling the arrival of the train from the East. The lawman drew up to the Rusty Lantern Saloon, and though the morning air had a bite to it, the double doors of the saloon were open, leaving only the batwings to pass through.

Iron knew Benny Wilson well. The youngest son of a prominent local rancher, he sometimes shot off his mouth when he got too much liquor in him. Iron had rescued him from a couple of beatings before, but this was the first time Benny was facing a gunfight.

A deep voice from inside abruptly called for Benny to draw. Iron burst into the saloon. His deputy was on his heels, and Stenzel caught the swinging doors and held them open. With the challenge issued, the place was gripped in silence, and the dozen or so patrons stood by wordlessly. Wilson himself, his head wobbly and his hands shaking from drink, had his back against the bar and was leaning against it to support himself. Fifteen feet away, his challenger stood between two tables in a slight crouch, his right hand hovering over the pearl handle of his holstered gun.

Will Iron recognized the dark, sullen man with hawklike features immediately. His name was Emmett Sandidge, and he was known to be fast and deadly. The intrusion by the sheriff had not pulled his attention from Wilson. His eyes were cold and implacable, like those of a diamondback rattler.

The sheriff stood just inside the door, and his voice cut across the thick silence. "Hold it right there, Sandidge!"

The gunslick kept his stance but turned his head

enough to gaze at Iron. He regarded the lawman with contempt, and his voice was full of disrespect as he said, "Butt out, Sheriff. This ain't none of your affair. This fool opened his trap one time too many. Now he's gonna draw against me."

Iron did not take his unwavering stare from the gunslinger, and his hand hung just over the butt of his Colt .45 as he addressed the sodden youth at the bar. "Benny, I want you out of here. Right now."

Sandidge bristled, a blaze of anger flaming his face. "He ain't goin' nowhere but to the graveyard, Iron! I told you to butt out!"

The lawman did not respond. "Benny . . . go!" he bellowed, bearing down hard on the final word.

Sandidge's chest rose and fell with the fury he was feeling. Lancing Iron with a hard glare, he warned, "If he walks out of here, I'll get him later—after I kill you, *old man*."

The gunslick's insult brought heat to Will Iron's blood. "He's walking out of here," the sheriff stated. "And we'll see just who kills whom."

Taking his cue, Benny Wilson quickly disappeared through the batwings. The small crowd of onlookers stood like wooden Indians.

Satisfied that the youth was safe, the sheriff said, "Now, Sandidge, the choice is yours. You can play the big, brave gunfighter and go for your weapon . . . or you can live till you meet your match in some other saloon. Choice is yours. Walk or draw."

The lawman flexed his fingers. He was certain he knew what Sandidge would decide. After all, the shooter had a reputation to uphold. Though he might well be feeling fear, he would not show it—and he would see through what he started. No doubt he was thinking that he was still several years shy of thirty, while Iron was close to twice his age. He was bound to figure he could take an aging lawman any day of the week.

The gunfighter's hand dipped for the weapon on his hip. But before Sandidge's weapon even cleared leather, Iron's gun was out and belching fire, and the slug slammed into the gunfighter just above his stomach. He buckled like a man struck with a battering ram, struggling with his gun and attempting to draw it free of its holster. Then his knees gave way, and he slumped to the floor.

The lawman took a few steps and stood over him. Sandidge looked up, a bewildered expression on his face. Blood spilled from between his lips as he worked his mouth, attempting to speak and looking dumbly at the sheriff through the gun smoke that filled the room. No sound ever came. His eyes closed and his body slumped. His hand, still gripping the gun butt, fell away.

Not a man in the Rusty Lantern moved until the sheriff's voice broke the spell. "Couple of you fellas carry him down to the undertaking parlor. County'll pick up the tab . . . as always."

Two of the men began hauling Sandidge away and several of the onlookers were disdaining the gunslinger's remark about Iron's age when the sheriff turned to leave and found a slender young tenderfoot standing wide-eyed in the doorway, looking over Jim Stenzel's shoulder. Clad in a business suit and a black derby hat, the young man rushed over to Iron and stuck out his hand. "Sheriff, that was some shooting! Oh, allow me to introduce myself. I'm Bernie Tripp. I arrived just before that fellow went for his gun . . . for the last time."

Iron assessed the clean-shaven, hollow-cheeked young reporter, who was about his height and had black hair and dark brown eyes. Shaking the proffered hand, he said, "So you're the fella from the *Police Gazette*. Pleasure to meet you. This is my deputy, Jim Stenzel."

The reporter removed his derby and shook hands with Stenzel. Tripp appeared to be a few years older than the deputy. As Emmett Sandidge's bloody corpse was carried through the door, Tripp eyed it with revulsion, then said to Iron, "I came here to interview you and then watch you work. I didn't think I'd see you in action so soon."

"Neither did I," Iron responded dryly. "Come on. Let's go to my office."

Five minutes later, the two lawmen sat down at their desks while the Easterner pulled over a chair and opened his briefcase. Pulling out a notebook, Tripp explained that he wanted to get Iron's complete background, including how he got into law enforcement.

"How long's this going to take?" Iron asked.

"These interviews usually last three or four hours."

The sheriff looked at his deputy and grinned. "Jim, if any minor problems arise while Mr. Tripp is taking notes about me, handle them, okay? It's not often I get the opportunity to go on about myself with such a willing listener."

Chuckling, Stenzel nodded his agreement, then leaned back in his chair and listened as Tripp began questioning Iron about his birthplace, his childhood, and the like.

About twenty minutes into the interview Stenzel saw a couple of riders pull up in front of the office, leading a third horse. The deputy caught only a glimpse of the animal but could see that something was tied to its back. The riders dismounted, and one of them called out, "Sheriff!"

Rising from his chair, Stenzel said, "I guess this is one of those minor things, Will. I'll take care of it."

Stepping out the door, the deputy recognized two

local ranchers, Jeff Armstrong and Wiley Binn. Their faces were grim. Stenzel's gaze then shifted to the load the third horse was carrying: It was a corpse. Stenzel immediately recognized young Billy Barton, his blood-soaked body riddled with bullets. Horrified, Stenzel swore softly and started to turn back toward the office door when Binn asked, "Is the sheriff in, Jim?"

Nodding, the deputy said, "I'm getting him." He stuck his head in the doorway and called, "Sheriff, I'm afraid this isn't a minor thing after all. Come out here quick!"

Bernie Tripp followed Will Iron outside, where a crowd was quickly gathering. The reporter's face blanched as he took in the gruesome sight of the body. He leaned against one of the posts that supported the porch roof and took a deep breath.

Clearly stunned, the sheriff examined young Barton's body. Armstrong leaned close to Iron and said in a low voice, "We counted nine bullets in him, Sheriff."

"Where'd you find him?" Iron asked grimly.

"About three miles south of town," Binn answered. "He was lying in a ditch just off the road, right by the spot where those four cottonwoods are clustered together."

Nodding, Iron said, "I know the spot."

Armstrong put a hand on the horse's left flank and said, "This here horse was grazing just a piece away. But this ain't Billy's animal, Sheriff. See there? The Bar-Q. That's Tom Quinn's brand."

Iron moved back a step, shook his head, and said, "Who'd want to do a thing like this to Billy? And what's he doin' on Tom's animal?"

"Doesn't make sense," Jim Stenzel put in.

"Maybe it'll make more sense when I talk to Tom," Iron said, sighing. "Poor kid. Never hurt anybody."

Dispatching Jim Stenzel for the undertaker, Iron told him to stop at the hardware store and inform Don

Nelson what had happened to his young clerk. Nelson was going to be terribly saddened, the lawman thought. He had become almost a surrogate father to Billy during the time the youth had worked for him.

With Bernie Tripp looking on wide-eyed, Iron discussed the murder with the two ranchers and speculated on the brutality of the crime. Minutes later, Don Nelson arrived. At the awful sight of young Barton's lifeless, bloodied body, Nelson went as white as a sheet. He told Iron that he had wondered why Billy had not come to work this morning. He thought perhaps the youth had taken ill during the night, but he had not had time to go to Billy's house and check on him.

Telling Nelson what little he knew, the sheriff said that he would head out to the Quinn ranch right away. "I'll fill you in on anything I learn as soon as I get back."

Nodding, Nelson stood silently staring at his young employee, returning to his store only after the undertaker took the body away in his funeral wagon.

Iron then turned to his deputy and said, "Jim, you mind the office. I'm going to take Tom's horse out to him and see what, if anything, he knows. I'll also stop and examine the spot where Billy was found. Maybe I can pick up a clue there."

"Sure thing, Will."

As Iron led Tom Quinn's horse toward the stable where he kept his own animal, his mind was occupied with the murder he had on his hands. He was suddenly aware that Bernie Tripp was walking beside him.

"Sheriff," the Easterner said, "my editor-in-chief told me to stick around Casper for a few days and watch you operate. Would you mind if I ride along with you to the Quinn ranch? I promise not to get in your way, and when we get back we can take up the interview where we left off."

Iron considered the idea for a moment, then replied, "I guess that'd be all right. You can rent a horse at the stable where I keep my mount." He walked on a few more steps, then stopped and eyed the reporter dubiously. "You *can* ride, can't you?"

Tripp smiled. "Yes, sir, I sure can. It just so happens that there's a fine riding academy in New York's Central Park."

"Trust me, Mr. Tripp. This will *not* be a stroll—or a ride, as the case may be—in the park. If you can't keep up, you get left behind. The safety of the people of Casper comes before your story."

The reporter nodded. "Don't worry, I'll keep up."

Chapter Three

Sheriff Will Iron and Bernie Tripp dismounted at the spot where Billy Barton had been shot to death. Scrutinizing the ground carefully, Iron found tracks belonging to a number of riders, but it was impossible to discern just which of them had been involved in the murder and which had merely been people passing by on the well-traveled road. Nothing at the scene of the crime gave him any clue that would lead him to the killers.

Returning to their saddles, they rode on toward the Bar-Q Ranch. As they left the road and turned onto Tom Quinn's land, Iron spotted the rancher high up on the framework of his windmill some sixty yards behind the barn. Quinn was working intently on the pumping mechanism and did not notice the visitors.

Dismounting at the corral gate, Iron and Tripp tied their horses to the pole fence, along with the horse that had carried Billy Barton to town earlier that morning. They walked around the corral and out into the field toward the windmill. As they drew near, the rancher looked down and saw them.

"Mornin', Sheriff," Quinn called down from his high perch. "Who's that you've got with you?"

"His name's Bernie Tripp, Tom," Iron replied, his gaze fixed on the man who towered far above him.

"He's a reporter for the *Police Gazette*. He's here to do a story on me, of all things."

"Oughtta make a good one," the rancher responded, chuckling. Meeting the reporter's gaze, he said, "Glad to meet you, Mr. Tripp. I'll be down in just a minute."

Quinn quickly finished his repair project, then worked his way down on the metal framework. When he reached the bottom, he pulled a rag from his hip pocket and began wiping the black grease from his hands. Grinning at the skinny reporter, he said, "I'd offer to shake hands with you, Mr. Tripp, but I'd advise against it."

Tripp merely smiled.

Quinn turned to Iron and said evenly, "I don't think you have time for social calls, Will, so that means this is business. What can I do for you?"

Pointing at the horses in the corral, Iron asked, "Were you aware that your chestnut gelding was missing?"

Looking surprised, the husky rancher replied, "Why, no. No, I wasn't. See, I always feed the horses at noon. I was going to do it right after I finished with the windmill. Where'd you find him?"

Quickly, Iron told Quinn the whole story. The rancher was stunned. "I just can't believe it," he declared. "Billy murdered! It just doesn't seem possible. And why would he take my horse?"

"I was hoping you could shed some light on this matter, Tom," said Iron, "but you're clearly as much in the dark as I am. Apparently Billy lost his own horse somewhere in these parts and took yours. Binn and Armstrong found his body about three miles south of town. Looks to me like he was attempting to get away from his killers."

As they talked more, the rancher led Iron and Tripp to the corral. Untying the chestnut, he led it through the gate and removed the bridle. The conversation continued as the sheriff and the reporter accompanied

Quinn inside the barn. The horses followed, knowing it was feeding time, and lined up at the feeding trough. Quinn went to the grain bin, took a scoop from a nail on the wall, and grabbed hold of the bin's lid. When he did, his eyes fell on the message scratched by Billy Barton. Gasping, he said, "Will! Look at this!"

With the reporter following him, the sheriff stepped to the bin and saw Billy's message.

After reading it, Iron felt sickened. He looked up at Quinn, whose face had paled. Clearly, the rancher was equally horrified by the message. The lawman's voice shook as he breathed, "Vic Maynard! I . . . I can't believe what I've just read."

Quinn nodded, then said slowly, "Will, I just remembered something. At sunup this morning I was on the front porch of the house when four of Vic's men rode by and waved to me. Let's see. It was Carl Leedom, J. P. Ayers, Lou Rippey, and . . . oh, yeah, Dean Dungan. They were coming from the north, heading toward the Circle M."

Bernie Tripp was busy taking notes.

Iron rubbed the back of his neck and mused, "In the four years that Vic has lived here, he's done so much for the community. The man has been more than generous with his money—and his reputation is impeccable. Why would a man like that murder two people, then have a third killed? How is it possible that he could even *be* a murderer?"

Shaking his head in disbelief, Quinn leaned against the feed bin, letting his eyes roam over Billy's writing. "I know it, Will. This has me totally stunned."

Iron ran his forefinger over the lettering, tracing out the words, almost as if he could feel what the dead youth had felt. "There's no way we can doubt Billy's words, Tom," he said softly. "He'd have no reason to lie . . . and somebody *did* kill him."

"It's spelled out pretty plain here," Quinn agreed. "You'll have to act on it."

Rubbing his chin, Iron said, "I'm going to ride out to the Tattens' place. If I find them shot to death, it'll leave no room for doubt. According to Billy's message, it was Vic who did the actual shooting. Since you saw Leedom, Dungan, Rippey, and Ayers coming from the direction where Billy's body was found this morning, they no doubt were his assassins. Billy's message says only that four men were chasing him. I'll have to have more than this before I arrest them for Billy's murder. But if the Tattens are dead, this message is enough for me to arrest Maynard."

The sheriff hurried out of the barn and over to his horse. He mounted up, as did the reporter, and as he settled in his saddle, Iron looked at Quinn and said, "Don't let anything happen to Billy's message, Tom. I'll need it for court evidence."

"I'll guard it with my life, Will," Quinn promised.

Putting their horses to a gallop, Iron and Tripp raced off. They arrived at the Tatten place within fifteen minutes, and when they rounded the corner of the house, they saw the two bodies sprawled on the ground near the back porch. Drawing rein, the lawman slid slowly from the saddle, feeling as though his insides had turned to stone. The Tattens had been shot and killed, just as Billy Barton had attested.

Iron turned to Tripp, who had also dismounted and was looking at the bodies, and said, "The way I figure it, the kid probably stumbled upon the scene just as the Tattens were being gunned down. He made a run for it. The four men then gave chase. Since Billy took Tom's horse, it's a safe bet that he probably had his horse shot from under him. He must have run the rest of the way in the dark, eluding them until he took the horse." He shook his head. "Then they spotted him and caught him."

The reporter looked away from the corpses and nodded. "I'd say that's a fair guess as to the way it happened, Sheriff."

Walking over to the porch, Iron stood over the Tattens and gritted his teeth. He was both furious and puzzled. Vic Maynard had done so much for the town and the county during the time he had lived there. Why would he murder the Tattens? And how could everyone—including himself—have been so fooled by the man?

Carl Leedom and Lou Rippey were about to ride out of a thick stand of cottonwood trees that stood behind the Tatten house and ride into the yard when they spotted the lawman and his companion. Abruptly reining in, Leedom whispered harshly, "It's Iron!"

Rippey's face paled. "Ain't nobody gonna convince me it's mere coincidence the sheriff happened to drop by the Tattens' place the mornin' after Vic killed 'em!" he rasped. "And if he knows about them bein' murdered, he probably also knows about the kid! Carl, I don't want to hang! I don't want to—"

"Shut up!" Leedom hissed, scowling. "They'll hear you!" Unnerved himself, he fought to stay in control, saying, "Don't panic, Lou. How could Iron have known the Tattens had been killed? Nobody knew about it but Vic and the five of us . . . and Billy Barton. It's certain none of us spilled it to anybody—and for *dead* certain the kid hasn't talked."

His words shaky, Rippey countered, "Well, he *does* know, Carl! He found out somehow! Maybe we just thought we killed the kid! Maybe somehow he lived to tell it!"

"There's no way that kid could have survived all them slugs, Lou. Now, get a grip on yourself. Maybe somebody just happened by this mornin' and found the Tattens. Like that stranger who's with Iron, maybe. That'd explain how Iron knows."

Rippey visibly relaxed. "Sure, that's it! So Vic's in the clear, and so are we."

"Yeah—if my theory's right." Leedom paused, then added, "But if Iron shows up at the Circle M, it'll mean my theory's wrong, and he knows who did it. Come on. Let's get back to Vic and tell him what's goin' on."

Being careful to stay out of sight, Leedom and Rippey walked their horses quietly out of the grove. As soon as they were out of earshot, they galloped away.

Will Iron and Bernie Tripp carried the bodies of John and Lucille Tatten into the house and placed them on the bed. As he was covering them with a blanket, the sheriff said, "I'll send the undertaker out to pick them up once I get back to town. Right now, I'm going to the Circle M Ranch and arrest Vic Maynard. According to Billy's note, the five ranch hands who were with Maynard didn't do the shooting, so I'll handle them later. Even though I'm sure the four that Tom Quinn mentioned seeing were the ones who ran down and murdered Billy, I'll have to dig up more proof before I arrest them and charge them. The first thing is to get Maynard behind bars."

Bernie Tripp followed the sheriff outside. As they drew near the horses, Iron instructed, "You go on back to town, and I'll look you up at the hotel when I'm ready to go on with the interview."

"Sheriff," Tripp said as he took hold of his horse's reins, "how about if I ride along with you to the Circle M?"

"Too dangerous," Iron replied, swinging into his saddle. "You go back to Casper."

Settling in his own saddle, Tripp argued, "But, Sheriff, my boss sent me here to get an eyewitness, first-hand account of your work. I need to see you in action, making an arrest."

Iron shook his head. "Maynard may put up a fight. He's got a whole passel of hired hands on the ranch. There could be gunplay—and you could get killed. I can't allow you to take that chance."

When Carl Leedom and Lou Rippey gave Vic Maynard the news that Will Iron was out at the Tatten place, the rancher felt as though an electric jolt had gone through his body. His beefy face turned white as he spat, "How could Iron have known the Tattens were shot? Didn't you guys make sure the Barton kid was dead?"

"The kid *was* dead when we left him, boss," Leedom said defensively. "We did our job right. There's no way the kid could have lived with as much lead as we put into him. In fact, the last shot went through his head. I put it there myself."

Maynard jabbed a finger at Leedom and demanded, "Then you tell me why Will Iron is at the Tatten place! It seems like too much of a coincidence that he'd just happen by there!"

Maynard and the two ranch hands were in the parlor of the ranch house. Leedom took a step backward, leaning against the windowsill. "I think I know why."

The rancher glared at him impatiently. "Well, spit it out!"

Leedom explained his theory of someone finding the bodies and then going into Casper to notify the lawman. "There was some stranger with Iron," the ranch hand said. "Looked like a tenderfoot."

Maynard nodded. "Well, that makes sense," he said in a more controlled voice, feeling relieved.

"So you see," Leedom concluded, "if that's the case,

there's no way you can be implicated in the Tattens' murder."

The rancher sighed, scrubbed a nervous palm over his face, and muttered, "Yeah. No way."

" 'Course, like I told Lou," Leedom added, "if that theory's wrong, then . . ."

Maynard's eyes narrowed. "Then what?"

"Well," Leedom said cautiously, "if we see Iron comin' in this direction, you can bet he knows who murdered the Tattens."

Maynard stiffened. "But that's an impossibility!" he blurted. "If the Barton kid was killed on the spot like you say, there's no way Iron can know I did it!"

"Boss," Lou Rippey suddenly put in, staring out the front window. "I think you should know that a rider's just left the road and is headin' this way." Rippey gasped. "It's Will Iron! I can tell by that light gray hat of his and the way he sits his horse!" He turned and stared at his employer, his eyes wide. "That means . . ."

Vic Maynard paled. Hurrying over to the window, he choked, "That means he's found out I killed the Tattens. He wouldn't have any other reason to come here." The rancher looked at his men. "I've got to get away! I'll go out the back way before he reaches the house. I'll have to ride hard and hole up somewhere so Iron doesn't find me. You two keep him busy here as long as you can to give me time to escape."

Rippey spoke up. "Why don't we just get rid of him like we got rid of the Barton kid? We can bury him somewhere on the far end of the property, and no one'll be the wiser."

Maynard shook his head. "You don't know what you're saying. Iron wouldn't kill easy. Lots of men have tried it—and lots of men are six feet under."

"But we've got him far outnumbered," Rippey argued. "I once heard tell that he took out six men at once, when they thought the same thing," countered the rancher. "No, I'll have to hightail it out of here while you guys think up something to tell him."

"Where you gonna go, boss?" Leedom asked.

"I don't know," Maynard answered, heading toward the back of the house. "You just sit tight until I show up again. Carl, I'm putting you in charge."

With that, Vic Maynard dashed out the back door of the house and ran toward the barn.

Chapter Four

Sheriff Will Iron rode in to the Circle M, ready to arrest Vic Maynard for murder. The lawman held his horse to a brisk walk as he made his way to the house past a huge barn, various outbuildings, and a large corral. The cowhands were busy working, though many of them stopped what they were doing to stare at him.

Hauling up at the front of the house, Iron dismounted, climbed the porch, and knocked on the door. When there was no response, he knocked a second time, louder and more insistently. The door opened and Carl Leedom emerged, followed by Lou Rippey.

"Howdy, Sheriff," Leedom said casually. "What can I do for you?"

"I'm here to see your boss," Iron replied, his voice hard.

"You seem awful grim, Sheriff," Leedom remarked, smiling unconvincingly. "Somethin' wrong?"

Ignoring the question, Iron said firmly, "I want to talk to Vic."

"He ain't here," Leedom responded with a shrug. "He left for California four days ago. Went to talk with some rancher out there about buying some special cattle. Gonna be gone quite some time, probably." He smiled again. "But if you tell me what it is you need to see Mr. Maynard about, well, maybe I can help you.

'Cause the fact of the matter is, he wasn't sure how long he'd be gone."

"Yeah," Rippey put in, "Mr. Maynard's a real good businessman. He heard about them cattle and decided that since this here operation's runnin' smooth enough, he could get away for a spell. Didn't say how long he was gonna be gone, but we told him not to worry, that we could handle whatever comes up."

Iron knew the men were lying and were covering their boss. Trying to unnerve them, the lawman abruptly said, "A double murder was committed not far from here. You men know anything about it?" The experienced lawman had been reading eyes and faces for many years, and he saw the truth in Leedom's and Rippey's eyes. But as he expected, the ranch hands lied.

"Murders!" Leedom exclaimed, eyeing his partner. "I haven't heard a thing about any murders, Sheriff. Anybody we know?"

"Yeah. John and Lucille Tatten."

Leedom's mouth dropped open. "John and Lucille murdered?"

"Yeah. Shot down like dogs in their own yard."

The ranch hands exchanged glances. "That's terrible," Leedom murmured. Looking back at Iron, he asked, "You got any idea who killed 'em?"

The sheriff wanted to blurt out that he knew Vic Maynard had done the shooting while Leedom and Rippey watched, but he checked himself. Calmly, he replied, "That's what I want to talk to Vic about."

Leedom shook his head. "Well, like I told you, Sheriff, he ain't here. If you have some reason to doubt my word, you can look the whole place over for yourself."

It was clear from Leedom's unconcerned demeanor that this part of his story was true. Maynard had obviously fled. Iron wished he had some idea as to when the rancher had left—it could have been anywhere from shortly after he had killed the Tattens, which apparently he'd done the day before, to ten minutes ago—but obviously he would get no help from Maynard's loyal employees. The rancher had eluded him, and there was nothing more Iron could do until he found him. He would have to start a search for the missing murderer immediately.

Staring coldly at the two ranch hands, Iron told them, in a voice filled with sarcasm, "Thanks for all your help."

He remounted his horse and rode back to town.

Bernie Tripp was waiting in the sheriff's office when Will Iron returned. "Did you get your man, Sheriff?" the reporter asked.

Iron shook his head. " 'Fraid not. Maynard had already left the ranch and gone into hiding. Since I don't know what kind of a head start he's gotten on me, I figure it might be some time before I catch him."

"You mean you're going on a manhunt?"

"That's exactly what I mean."

Tripp grinned. "Great! Now I'll really get to see you in action."

The lawman stared at the reporter as if he had lost his mind. "You're not going anywhere . . . unless it's back to New York. It's too dangerous. And on top of that, you're a city boy. Tracking a fugitive through those mountains is no picnic. It's plenty rough. A man has to be used to that kind of thing or it'll do him in. You couldn't take it."

"Maybe I'm tougher than I look," Tripp retorted, disappointment showing on his face.

"Maybe so," Iron argued, "but you're a reporter, not a lawman. You don't belong out in the wilds, hunting down criminals."

"But what about my story? My editor's going to be real angry if I don't come back with a good, solid interview."

Iron shrugged. "Can't be helped."

"Tell you what, Sheriff," said Tripp. "We could probably squeeze in the interview while we were traveling if you'd let me go along with you."

Iron shook his head. "Nope," he said flatly. "It's just too dangerous. Besides, you might get in my way and hinder me from doing what I have to do. Never know what kind of circumstances will develop."

"But—"

"No buts, Mr. Tripp. If you're still here when I get back—whenever that'll be—we'll finish the story. Or you can take the next train back to New York. The choice is yours. And those are the *only* choices you have. Now, if you'll excuse me, I've got to gather the town councilmen together and let them know what's going on."

After a dejected-looking Bernie Tripp left the office, heading for his hotel, the sheriff instructed his deputy to round up half of the council members while he got the others. They all met back at the office a half hour later, and the senior lawman filled everyone in on what had happened and what he intended to do.

When Iron had concluded his briefing, Ty Miller, the council chairman, suggested, "Will, I don't think you ought to go after Vic alone. It's hard to imagine that he's actually murdered two people, but since you're convinced that he's the one who did it, well, he's obviously either gone crazy or he's a killer by instinct. Either way, he's no doubt plenty desperate. I think you ought to form a posse and not go out after him alone."

"Posses are for chasing men on the prairie, out in the open, Ty," Iron said. "I've given it some thought, and I'm convinced that he headed up into the mountains, maybe planning to hole up and try to stay hidden. A posse's noisy; he'd hear it coming well in advance and have plenty of time to get away. No, it's best for me to go alone. I can be more efficient that way."

The councilmen were fully aware that Will Iron knew more about tracking criminals than all of them put together. Miller backed off, saying, "Well, you know best, so I'll leave it up to you." He looked at his fellow councilmen. "What about the rest of you?" he asked.

The others agreed.

"Okay, then that's settled," Iron stated. "And I'm sure you all feel as I do that there's no one more trustworthy to take over as sheriff while I'm gone than Jim. He's proven himself over and over by now."

The council members agreed that Stenzel would be acting sheriff of the county while Iron was off pursuing the murderer. Then they left the office, giving the two lawmen a chance to confer for a while.

"Have the undertaker go out for the Tattens' bodies, Jim," Iron advised. "And try to find out if they have any kin that need to be notified."

"I'll take care of it, Will," Stenzel assured him.

Taking a shotgun down from the gun rack, Will Iron clapped Jim Stenzel on the shoulder. "You're in charge of the county now, my boy."

The deputy nodded. "That's right. So don't you worry about anything but finding Vic Maynard. Good luck, Will. And be careful."

"Oh, I will. I've got a lot to come back to." With that, the sheriff headed back out to his horse, the shotgun cradled in his arm.

His saddlebags slung over his shoulder, Will Iron entered through the back door of his house and found his wife scrubbing the kitchen floor on her hands and knees. "Will!" Vanessa exclaimed, quickly standing up and wiping her soapy hands on her apron. "Has something happened? The only time you ever come home in the middle of the day is if something's wrong."

Sighing, Iron told her about the three murders and that he was about to go out in pursuit of the man responsible for them—Vic Maynard.

Vanessa's eyes widened, and she clutched the back of a chair for support. "Three people have been murdered, gunned down in cold blood, and Vic Maynard is responsible?" she said in an astonished voice. "I don't believe it."

"Neither did I at first, but I'm afraid it's true. Or at least he personally pulled the trigger on John and Lucille. Then he had his men take care of Billy."

Vanessa's face was white. She stared blankly at her husband for a long moment, then murmured, "But Vic Maynard has been so generous to this town. He gave half the money to build the schoolhouse, and he practically paid for the new church building all by himself. I've also heard that he's paid medical bills for people who otherwise couldn't have afforded proper medical attention. And we've never had any trouble from any of the men who work at the Circle M. Will, this just doesn't make any sense. Are you sure of what you're saying?"

"I wish it weren't true, sweetheart," the lawman said, laying a strong hand on her shoulder. "But it is. And I've got to catch him before he gets away." While he packed ammunition, food, and cooking gear into his saddlebags for his trek into the mountains, he explained to her how he knew that Maynard was guilty.

He finished packing and was buckling up his saddlebags when the redhead put her hand on her husband's arm and said, "Will, I wish you wouldn't go after Vic by yourself. Won't you please take some men with you?"

"As I told the town council, I'll have a better chance of catching him in the mountains on my own."

Knowing better than to argue with her husband, Vanessa nodded and said quietly, "Well, then, be careful."

Iron took his wife in his arms and said into her ear, "Of course I will. I've got a lot to live for." He kissed her soundly and released her. Tossing the heavy saddlebags over his shoulder and picking up his shotgun, he headed for the door.

"Will!" Vanessa called. "Here. You'll need these."

He smiled and took the matches from her, shoving them into his pants pocket. "You're right. I will."

Vanessa followed him out onto the porch, gave him another kiss, and wished him good luck.

"Thanks, darlin'," he said softly. "Tell the kids that I love them and I'll be back as soon as I can."

"I will," she promised.

Striding purposefully to his horse, Iron slung the saddlebags behind the saddle, secured them, and mounted up. He turned and looked back at the house, and as he expected, Vanessa was still standing there, watching him intently. He gave her a brief wave, then kneed his mount.

Once on the street, he rode south out of Casper, heading for the Circle M spread, where he hoped to pick up Maynard's trail. Iron's tracking skills were legendary, and he was able to read sign that most other men failed to see. Depending on the terrain, he looked for imprints in sod and grass, stones and pebbles disturbed or sometimes overturned so that their damp side was exposed, broken limbs on bushes or fallen leaves pressed into the ground, twigs snapped, and sometimes things dropped by a careless man that gave evidence that he had been there.

The lawman smiled to himself as he recalled following one outlaw who had been very careful not to leave tracks. But the man had been a tobacco chewer, and he had had to spit regularly. All the lawman had to do was follow the little brown smears on the ground and rocks and he had caught up to the owlhoot in no time. Iron shook his head, telling himself he could only hope that Vic Maynard had been as careless—and would therefore be as easy to find.

The sheriff was so intent on what lay ahead of him that, ironically, he completely disregarded his back trail . . . and so he was unaware that another rider was following him at a distance.

Having climbed into the foothills of the Rockies, Vic Maynard guided his exhausted, sweating horse into a thick stand of aspen and dismounted. He had never been so glad as he was now that he routinely carried a pair of binoculars in his saddlebags. Taking out the field glasses, he hurried to the edge of the aspens and checked his back trail. He carefully scanned the vista for a couple of minutes, finally deciding that, so far, no one was following.

After walking his mount around for a few minutes to cool the animal down, Maynard mounted once again, muttering to himself that, without a doubt, Will Iron was going to come. The fugitive pushed the horse hard once again, riding for an hour, following a stream that flowed from the lofty peaks above him. When he reached a shelf along the steep incline, he dismounted and climbed to the top of a huge boulder. The wind plucked at his hat and clothing as he again scanned his back trail with the binoculars.

Maynard saw no sign of a pursuer. Relieved, he was about to return to his horse when he caught sight of something moving amid the tall timber far below. He swung the glasses back to the spot where he had seen the movement, but there was nothing. Had he imagined it? No. He was certain that though nothing was there now, he had not imagined it. Something had moved down there in the shadows, and it was right where he had been when he had first started the steep climb.

Keeping the binoculars trained on the spot, he waited. After about a minute he saw movement again. *Yes!* he exclaimed to himself. *I knew it! Something did move down there.*

Presently a horse and rider came into view, duplicating Maynard's passage. The rancher's hands shook as he watched through the glasses, the rider—though still a long way off—getting steadily closer. *It's you, isn't it, Will? You're coming after me, aren't you? You're determined to get me.*

Less than five minutes passed before he was able to discern that the rider was a slender, middle-aged man sitting ramrod-straight in the saddle, wearing a light gray hat. Then a ray of afternoon sun gleamed off a badge on the man's chest. Seconds later the rider's features came into focus.

It was Will Iron, all right. The West's most determined and proficient lawman was coming after him! The friendship they had shared would make no difference to Iron. Maynard had murdered two Natrona County citizens and had sent four of his men to kill the innocent youth who had witnessed it. No mercy would be shown. The sheriff would take him in and see him hanged.

Panic struck.

What could Maynard do? He decided there was only one course of action: He would have to outwit and outsmart the seemingly invincible lawman. His mind raced. *I must find a way to kill Will Iron!*

Maynard slid quickly down the side of the rough,

towering boulder and dashed to his horse. As he stuffed the binoculars back in the saddlebag he said aloud, "The man is made out of flesh just like me. He's kept alive by a heartbeat the same as me. If my heart can be stopped, so can his. If I don't kill him, he'll take me back to hang. I can't let that happen. That'd destroy my kids."

Swinging into the saddle, the killer rode for higher country, feeling more confident now that he knew he would be the one to come out alive. His certainty fed by delusion, which in turn was fueled by his growing desperation, Maynard mulled over how he would accomplish his goal—escaping the long arm of the law. Surely by now everybody in and around Casper knew that he had murdered the Tattens, and Carl and the others who killed Billy Barton were probably already in jail. That meant he could never go back to his ranch. After he killed Iron, he would head north to Canada and lose himself in that remote country. He would explain away his move to his family by telling them that he had tired of Wyoming and wanted a change. Somehow he would start anew in ranching and he would convince his children to move up there with him. They would never know what he had done; they *could* not know. The shame of it would ruin them, and that he could not bear.

As he rode for higher country, Maynard rebuked himself for not coming clean with Martha about his past before he married her. Then he remembered how he had contemplated doing so but feared that if she knew that he was an ex-convict, she would have called off the wedding—and he had loved her too much to have chanced that happening.

The rancher pushed his horse hard up the steep trail, trying to think of a way to kill his pursuer. Presently he came to a jumbled pile of large rocks, and he was struck by an idea. Pulling rein, he carefully studied the position of the rocks. It appeared that they were precariously balanced, and if one of them was dislodged, it would let loose all of them—tons of rock spilling down the trail he had just climbed. His mind began racing. If he could time things just right, he could bury the sheriff forever.

Dismounting, Maynard looked around, then grabbed a sturdy tree limb that was lying nearby. He hurried over to the rock pile, jammed the larger end of the limb under the front rock, and wiggled it, using it as a fulcrum. The wind lashed his face as he struggled with the limb, but he ignored his discomfort. After a few moments Maynard felt something give, and the rock slid an inch or so. His heart beat faster. His plan would work!

Leaving the limb in place under the rock, Maynard began to pace, feeling a jumble of anticipation, fear, and regret. In a matter of minutes he could be rid of the lawman and make good his escape. He would be safe, and—more important—his children and grandchildren would be spared shame and heartbreak.

He stopped pacing. As he waited for Iron to appear he picked up his binoculars, and a chilling look settled on his face. The fugitive was unaware that something inside him had snapped. His once innate sense of morality had been irrevocably corrupted by his desperation and replaced by ruthlessness.

After what seemed an eternity Maynard finally saw the lawman coming up the side of the mountain, carefully studying the trail for sign. Watching the slow ascent of his pursuer, Maynard murmured, "That's it, Will, my friend. Your old pal Vic has a surprise for you. I'm gonna be your executioner, and your undertaker as well. You've left me no choice. Too bad there won't be a preacher to say some nice words over your grave."

Putting the binoculars away, Maynard moved to the rock and took hold of the limb. His body tingled with anticipation as he watched and waited.

Nearly a half hour passed before Iron reached just the right spot below: a narrow passage between two granite walls. Maynard grunted heavily as he threw all his weight onto the tree limb, freeing the pivotal rock. Once it was dislodged, the others behind it were set free, and, with a thunderous roar, tons of rocks bounded down the mountain, hurtling toward the sheriff.

Defying Sheriff Will Iron, Bernie Tripp had followed the lawman out of Casper, keeping well back on his rented horse. The *Police Gazette* reporter had reasoned that if he maintained a good distance, Iron would not be aware of his presence, but by keeping the lawman just barely in sight, Tripp would be able to see him when he caught up to Vic Maynard—and he himself could then catch up and see the capture firsthand. His story would have real punch if he could describe the action as he had seen it with his own eyes. So what if he took a tongue-lashing from Iron? That's all the sheriff could do. And to get an eyewitness account to report would be worth it.

By the time they entered the tall timber, Tripp had closed the gap somewhat, carefully staying about a hundred and fifty yards behind the sheriff, who was intently reading Maynard's sign as he inched his horse up the steep trail. As the climbing became more difficult, Tripp's horse was wheezing and snorting with effort, and the reporter decided he should let the animal rest. Reaching a level spot a few yards ahead, Tripp slid from the saddle. "There now, fella," he said, patting the horse's rump. "You take a breather while I keep an eye on the sheriff."

Now, the wind whipping across the mountain tugged

at Tripp's clothing and threatened to pluck away his derby. Pulling the hat tighter on his head, he watched the movements of the lawman far above him, certain that though he had not yet caught sight of Maynard, Iron knew how much farther ahead the killer was.

Suddenly Tripp's attention was drawn to a flash of movement some fifty yards above the sheriff. It was Maynard! It took him a moment to figure out what the killer was doing, but as he squinted and studied the man's movements, it became evident that Maynard was attempting to create a rockslide.

Tripp looked quickly back at Iron. From the way the lawman was riding, it was obvious that he was unaware of what was happening. Perhaps the shape of the mountain effectively blocked Maynard from the sheriff's view.

Then it happened. The rocks began careening downward straight at Iron, now trapped between two high granite walls. Gasping, Tripp cupped his hands and shouted a warning . . . but he knew even as he did it that it was too late.

Chapter Five

Sheriff Will Iron had guided his horse about a third of the way through the granite-walled passage when he became aware of what at first sounded like thunder. Looking up, he felt his blood freeze. Raining down on him were not droplets of water but hundreds of rocks!

Acting instinctively, the seasoned lawman jerked his mount's head around, attempting to turn it in the close quarters, but the oncoming rocks terrified the animal, and it whinnied and balked. The more Iron shouted at the horse and tried to make it turn and run, the more it fought the bit in its mouth.

Iron spotted a cleft some four feet wide and little more than two feet deep in the side of the granite wall to his left. Knowing he had only seconds to escape, Iron leapt from the saddle, but the jerky movements of his frightened horse caused him to slip, and he went down hard, striking his left knee on a sharp rock. Pain shot through his leg like daggers of fire as he staggered into the shallow depression. Flattening himself as best he could, he clung to the narrow niche, feeling it tremble as the rocks hurtled closer, drowning out his horse's screams of terror. Iron hung on as tons of rock rumbled past him and enveloped him in a cloud of brown dust.

It seemed as though the rocks would never stop coming. Then as suddenly as the rockslide had started, it stopped. Iron continued to hug the wall at the back of the cleft, and it was only after the dust had blown away that he turned and looked. Rubble was heaped up in the narrow passageway. If the slide had lasted much longer, he would have been buried alive in the cleft. He knew his horse had been killed. There was no way the poor animal could have survived.

His knee was throbbing horribly. He would give it a few minutes' rest before trying to climb out of the passageway. Then, despite what he feared might be a broken kneecap—and until he could somewhere, somehow procure another horse—he would have to follow Maynard on foot.

Up above, Vic Maynard felt a momentary pang of guilt as the dust blew away and he saw two legs of Iron's horse sticking out from under the pile of dirt and rocks. But then he thought of what would have happened if Iron had lived, and all compassion vanished. He laughed victoriously and called out, "Nice touch, don't you think, Will? Being buried with your horse? Now the two of you can be together for all eternity."

Still chuckling, Maynard turned and walked to his own horse. "Well, boy," the killer said as he mounted up, "now you don't have to carry me any higher up these mountains. We can head back down now and hightail it to safety without worrying about being followed."

Suddenly Maynard shook his head, muttering, "Just how did Iron find out I was responsible for the murders? The Tattens were dead. Billy Barton was dead. . . ." He stiffened. "That leaves my men," he growled. "One of them turned traitor, that's what happened! Yeah! That's it! One of those men I stupidly trusted turned against me! Probably one of the four I sent after the Barton kid, since Ed Kruse never left my sight. Or maybe it was all four of 'em! Or . . . or maybe they lied to me. Maybe they didn't kill the kid at all!"

Maynard pondered that possibility. The more he thought about it, the more it made sense. Sure. If he was out of the picture, his foreman, Carl Leedom, could get the ranch. Leedom knew the ranch was willed to the Maynard children, so all he had to do was open the safe at the house and destroy the will. "The dirty skunk never killed Billy Barton at all," the rancher grumbled. That being the case, the law would have no reason to want Leedom or the other three.

That had to be it. After all, they had had no idea their boss was planning to kill the Tattens when they rode into their yard. His men had been taken by surprise when Maynard pulled his gun, and he had already shot the Tattens before they could have had any time to do anything about it. Billy would be right there to testify that when he had ridden up, it was Vic Maynard who was gunning down the helpless couple.

A cleverly conceived plan. Leedom and the others had set him up. Made up a tale about some stranger in a derby hat and an Easterner's clothes having been the one who had led Iron to the Tattens' bodies. That was just a stall. Leedom had known all along that Iron was on his way to the ranch to arrest Maynard, and it had been just an act when he and Rippey acted shocked to see Iron heading for the house.

Hatred burned in the rancher toward the men he had so recently felt so obliged to. They were nothing but traitors looking to steal his wealth. Maynard wanted to go back and kill every one of them—but revenge would have to wait. Nothing was worth taking the chance of getting caught and stretching a rope. Someday, when the law had forgotten about him—when his men figured they were sitting pretty—he would come back and make them pay for what they had done to him.

As he swung into the saddle, Maynard thought about the fortune he had on deposit at the Casper bank. It grieved him that he could not even draw out his money. He swore loudly. No doubt Leedom would find a way to get his hands on that, too. Nudging his horse, the fugitive guided it back the way he had come.

Down below, Will Iron heard Maynard laughing, but he could not make out the words. Deciding the pain in his knee had subsided about as much as it was going to, the lawman began to climb over the rubble. He scrambled slowly, doing his best to ignore the stabbing pain, but not succeeding. Reaching the top of the pile, he saw his horse's legs poking out of the pile of rocks and dirt. His heart was heavy. The animal had served him faithfully for the past four years.

Staring at the tons of debris that covered most of the horse, Iron knew it would be impossible to dig out his shotgun and the saddlebags. He was now without food and supplies. Moreover, he had just six bullets in his revolver and twenty-four in the loops on his gun belt. He had no idea how well armed Maynard was.

The pain in Iron's knee was excruciating, but he limped around the heap of rubble and began making his way through the brush and boulders. Once again he was climbing the mountain on Vic Maynard's trail.

Weaving his way down the mountain, Vic Maynard suddenly jerked back on the reins, his eyes bulging and his blood turning to ice. At first he thought he was looking at some horrible apparition—but, no, the man was real. Will Iron was climbing toward him on foot. Because of the angle and the steep ascent, the lawman had not spotted him, and Maynard could not tell his pursuer was limping.

The killer asked himself how Iron could have possibly

escaped being buried in the rockslide. Certainly his horse had not escaped it. Cursing his rotten luck, Maynard yanked hard on the reins to turn his horse around and began climbing once more.

Some forty yards separated them when Iron, spotting his prey just as Maynard was pivoting his animal, shouted, "Vic! Hold it right there!"

The muscles in the killer's face twitched. Holding the reins tight with his left hand, he whipped out his revolver with the right and began firing at Iron. But the sheriff dived for cover, ducking behind a boulder while slugs chipped uselessly at the rock, whining shrilly as they ricocheted away.

Then Maynard's gun clicked hollowly, its shells spent. Iron cautiously stood up and shouted, "Give it up, Vic! I'll get you sooner or later anyhow! Spare yourself the trouble of trying to get away!"

Desperate to put as much distance as possible between them as quickly as possible, Maynard cursed the lawman, shoved the empty gun back into its holster, and spurred his horse up the steep slope into the dense timber. As he rode through the deep shade of the towering conifers, the fugitive laughed. There was no way Will Iron was going to catch him on foot.

The killer continued ever higher until suddenly he was faced with a perilously steep incline. Looking to his right, he decided to ride along a natural shelf that lay in that direction. Even though it was lateral movement, he was still getting farther from his determined pursuer, and that was all that mattered.

He had gone less than sixty feet when he came to a crevasse in the face of the mountain. Maynard knew he could jump across it, but he would never get the horse to make the leap. Wheeling the animal around, he headed back. He would try the other direction. But when he reached the spot where he had been before and started to the left, he saw that that passage was even more precarious than the route he had already tried. A quick glance below showed the lawman heading straight toward him. Maynard's horse would have to climb the steep slope after all.

Spurring the animal, Maynard aimed it up the precipitous grade, made even more treacherous because it was covered with pieces of shale. The horse snorted and balked, but Maynard swore at it, gouged its sides savagely with his spurs, and whipped it mercilessly. The frightened animal sprang upward. They had gone about twenty feet when the horse lost its footing, slipping sideways, and its leg fall into a thin crevice, breaking with a sickening snap.

Shouting a string of profanities over the horse's pitiable whinnying, Maynard sprang from the saddle. He left the poor beast to suffer and kept climbing on foot.

Will Iron could not tell exactly what had happened, but he spotted his quarry suddenly heading into the timber on foot and presumed Maynard had lost his mount. Doing his best to ignore the pain in his leg, Iron continued his climb as fast as possible.

Three times the agony of his injured knee drove the lawman to a halt. Each time he gave himself just a few moments' respite, then forced himself to continue. Soon he reached the place where Maynard's horse was stuck in the crevice. His experienced eye quickly told him that the leg was broken. Knowing the animal was doomed and hating to see anything suffer, Iron pulled his Colt .45, thumbed back the hammer, and said, "I'm sorry to have to do this, old boy, but I've no other choice." Aiming between the horse's eyes, he pulled the trigger. The horse died instantly.

With the echo of the shot clattering over the rocky

face of the mountain, the lawman pushed upward, glad to know that his man was now also on foot.

Higher up, Vic Maynard heard the shot and flinched. Looking back, he decided the shot was not meant for him after all; it was Will Iron putting the horse out of its misery. Gauging the distance between himself and his hunter by the sound, Maynard decided he could rest for a few moments. His mouth was bone-dry; it was so hard to breathe that his lungs hurt, and he was starting to feel nauseated from the exertion—exertion he was not at all used to and that his overweight body was ill-equipped for.

But after a few moments' rest Maynard was struck by a mental picture of himself with a rope around his neck and a black hood being dropped over his head. He visualized his four children clutching his grandchildren, all their faces filled with horror—or was it disgust? Telling himself he must not allow the sheriff to catch him, he forced his aching, exhausted body on.

By late afternoon the killer had been pushing himself for two hours with hardly a letup. Finally, his legs gave out. Finding a flat rock beneath a stand of aspens, he sat down, his breathing ragged and labored and his heart hammering. He had hardly sat down when the nausea that had been clawing at his stomach suddenly assaulted him, and he fell to his knees, his body wracked with dry heaves. Retching and gagging till the nausea had passed and his strength was gone, he shakily reached for the rock and sat down again.

When his breathing became more normal, he stood up and looked down the treacherous trail he had been covering. Far below, the tenacious lawman was still coming. Maynard cursed him, then abruptly felt a horrible new sensation in his chest. Sharp pains began to shoot from shoulder to shoulder, and he folded like an accordion, whimpering. Was his heart going to fail? He had experienced slight pains in his chest now and then over the last few years, but they had not alarmed him.

This pain was fierce, and he felt a tingling throughout his body. Cold sweat beaded his brow. Never had he been so frightened. Was he going to die up here on this mountain? He could not let that happen. Will Iron would take his body back to Casper, then contact his children in Nebraska, telling them that their father had died trying to escape arrest for murder.

"No!" he gasped. "No!"

Abruptly the pain subsided somewhat, almost as if he had willed it. Still doubled over, he waited, hardly daring to believe that the pain would not return in force. But it continued as just a dull ache, and his relief was immense. He rose to his feet and checked on Iron. The sheriff was still climbing—*like a mountain lion*, the killer told himself, *closing in for the kill*.

Panic once again gripped the fugitive, and he looked up, contemplating his escape route. He squinted. What appeared at first to be just a dark blotch in the trees was in fact the mouth of a cave—the perfect place to hide while he gave his body some much-needed rest. Removing bullets from his gun belt, he reloaded his revolver. When Iron reached the cave, as he was bound to do, he would taste slugs from Maynard's gun.

Summoning every ounce of strength he could muster, the killer climbed up to the cave. When he reached it, he paused at the opening. Breaking open his revolver, he checked that it was fully loaded, then holstered it. He caught sight of the sheriff threading his way among the trees and boulders below, getting closer, and hurried into the cave. Sitting on the cool, damp earth, his presence obscured by darkness, Maynard leaned against the rock wall as he waited. His position gave him a perfect view of the ground outside. When the lawman approached, he would get a bellyful of lead.

Vic Maynard ruminated angrily about his situation. He hated being on the defensive, he hated having to be on the run . . . and he hated Will Iron for making him feel like a hunted animal.

Limping badly, sweating from pain and exertion in the thin mountain air, Sheriff Iron continued doggedly upward. He was grateful at least that Vic Maynard was a heavy man, and that a great deal of his bulk was fat. It would slow him down pretty soon—and when it did, Iron would capture him.

Arriving at the flat rock where Maynard had rested, the sheriff discerned signs in the soft earth that told him the man had been on his knees. Had Maynard been praying? Or was he so exhausted that he had fallen to his knees?

Following the killer's footprints, Iron soon spotted the cave and realized that Maynard had taken refuge in the dark aperture in the side of the mountain. The sheriff had faced situations like this in the past and knew that the fugitive was waiting in there to shoot from the darkness. But he had a surprise for Maynard. Digging into his pocket, he fished out the box of matches, thankful that their last-minute addition meant they had not been put in his saddlebag. He would smoke Maynard out. Such a ploy had worked before; there was no reason to think it would not work again.

Careful not to make himself a target, Iron limped out of sight of the cave and began wadding a ball of dry weeds and twigs. When the ball was of sufficient size, he poked a slim branch loosely into it, then shouldered the makeshift "weapon" as he worked his way closer to the cave. When he was satisfied with his position, he lit a match and set fire to the ball of weeds dangling from the end of the branch. As soon as it was burning well, he slung it hard, catapulting it into the cave.

"Toss your gun out, Maynard, then come out with your hands in the air!" the sheriff shouted. Backing away so as to have a good angle on the killer when he came out, Iron waited, gun in hand. But when he heard no coughing and Maynard did not appear, he swore under his breath. Apparently there was another way out of the cave.

While smoke billowed out of the large opening, Iron noticed that, higher up, thin tendrils were rising toward the sky. Sure enough, there *was* another exit, and Maynard had obviously found it.

Breathing another oath, the sheriff holstered his revolver. Maynard had been mighty lucky that this cave had more than one entrance—but his luck was eventually going to run out. Will Iron would see to that.

He started walking, and his effort was rewarded with a sharp pain in his left leg. Gritting his teeth, the determined lawman kept climbing. The chase was not over yet.

Chapter Six

A pair of chipmunks scurried over the rubble from the rockslide as Bernie Tripp reined in and stared in disbelief. The reporter's heart sank when he saw the legs of Iron's horse sticking out from beneath the pile of rocks and dirt. Dismounting slowly, he pictured the sheriff's body crushed and lifeless under the tons of rubble. It would be impossible to dig the corpse out. Will Iron would remain interred where he had died.

Tripp thought about Vic Maynard. First the man had murdered the Tattens and had his men kill the boy; now Maynard had taken Sheriff Iron's life. The rancher deserved to hang, but Bernie Tripp was unarmed and lacking the know-how and experience to capture criminals.

Staring at the rubble, Tripp said aloud, "I'm really sorry your life had to end like this, Sheriff. We all have to die, but a man of your caliber deserved to die with more dignity than this. I promise you one thing: You're going to get the best article any lawman ever got in the *Police Gazette*. You'll go down in history as a real hero. Yes, sir, I'm going to—"

A gunshot rang out, coming from higher up on the mountain. Tripp's head jerked up and he scanned the tree-covered slopes, but he saw no one. The reporter was puzzled. Was it Vic Maynard doing the shooting? If so, whom was he shooting at? Certainly not at Tripp. The shot had been at too high a level to be meant for him.

Tripp's rented horse danced nervously. Patting its neck, he murmured, "What is it, fella? Do you know something I don't?"

The horse grew quiet. Tripp took off his derby and used it to shade his eyes from the glare of the sun as he carefully ran his gaze over the steep slopes above him. A few birds wheeled in the sky and others chattered in the trees, but there was no sign of anything human. He waited for a few more minutes, thinking there might be another gunshot, but when nothing happened, he mounted up. "Well, time to go, boy. We've got to get back to town and tell them what happened up here."

Tripp guided the horse back down the trail, letting the animal pick its way slowly on the steep, rocky spots. When he had ridden for a while, he came to an open area and glanced casually over his shoulder, almost as if bidding the place—and Will Iron—farewell. To his surprise he saw what appeared to be a man heading up the mountain. Then the figure disappeared into the trees.

Shading his eyes again, Tripp intently studied the area around where the figure had been. Suddenly he caught sight of the man again, climbing higher still. The man's light gray Stetson was like a beacon as he wove into the sunlight from the shade.

"It's Iron!" the reporter gasped. "He's alive! How on earth . . . ? Oh, who cares how? He's alive and chasing that killer on foot!"

There was no sign of Vic Maynard, but Tripp knew Iron was on his trail. He was certain now that the gunshot he had heard meant one of them had taken a shot at the other. Tripp wondered why a return shot had not been fired.

The Easterner's mind was working fast. He wanted to

help the sheriff, but he was fearful that Iron would be angry at him for following against his orders. After thinking about it for a moment, the reporter decided to take the chance. He would catch up to Iron and tell him they could ride double on the rented horse.

Breathing hard and limping badly, Sheriff Will Iron pressed on. He discovered Vic Maynard's escape route from the cave, a narrow passageway that came out on the far side of the slope. Though Iron had spotted Maynard several times during the climb, the fugitive was out of sight for the moment.

Iron was exhausted. His tongue and throat begged for water. He could hear a waterfall splashing somewhere nearby, but the echo effect in the mountains made it difficult to pinpoint its location. Cocking his head, he listened closely, finally deciding it was somewhat above him, off to his right. The sound of the moving water intensified his thirst.

Iron took a deep breath, steeled himself against the pain that came from his knee whenever he moved, and began climbing toward the sound of the falling water. Gripping his knee as he walked, he passed through a stand of windblown lodgepole pines, climbed over a ridge, and at last found a shallow ravine with a gurgling brook at its bottom. Smiling with relief, the sheriff limped down the side of the ravine and hunkered down at the edge of the stream. Pulling off his Stetson, he plunged his head into the cold water, leaving it there a few seconds as he let its icy fingers stimulate his face. He pulled his head out, gasping for air, and then began to drink. When his thirst was quenched, he shook the water from his salt-and-pepper hair and redonned his hat.

Feeling somewhat refreshed and eager to get back on Maynard's trail, Iron stood up, wiped his face with his sleeve, and took a deep breath. When he had worked his way back up to the edge of the ravine, he ran his gaze across the face of the mountain above him. It took a few moments, but he finally caught a glimpse of his prey, shuffling along a rock-topped ridge. "Okay, Maynard," he muttered. "Go ahead, run. But you have my solemn promise that I'm going to get you."

Within seconds, Maynard had disappeared over the lip of the ridge. Iron followed in little more than a shambling walk, his injury not permitting anything faster than that. Every pounding footstep was agonizing, sending shock waves of pain through his whole body, but he could not let it halt his pursuit. The Tattens' killer had to be brought to justice. With that done, Iron would then concentrate on the vermin who had murdered Billy Barton. They would not get away with it, either.

Iron thought about his family, especially his wife. Undoubtedly, Vanessa was worrying about him; she always did when he went after a criminal. For that matter, she worried every day that he pinned on his badge, strapped on his gun belt, and headed for the office—but not once had she ever complained. He was a lawman when she married him, and she had known what she was getting into.

What she did not seem to realize was that she was worrying unnecessarily about a slowdown in his reflexes. Iron knew his own body better than anyone and knew his reflexes were just about the same as always. Of course, the day *would* eventually come when his reflexes slowed, and then he would turn in his badge and hang up his gun. But he figured he had a good five years before that happened. Maybe even more.

The air was getting thinner as Iron climbed, and his lungs were complaining. He caught another glimpse of Maynard and realized the fugitive was moving as slowly as he. Sure, he had a badly injured knee, but otherwise he was in excellent shape; the rancher was hauling around excess weight, on a body grown soft. Maynard was obviously growing weary. His head-start advantage was rapidly diminishing; the gap was narrowing. It would not be much longer now.

Iron had to stop and give his lungs a chance to rest. His knee needed a break even more. It had swollen a great deal, and the pain had become unbearable. Moving into a more densely treed area, the lawman spotted a fallen log. Sitting, he sighed wearily and began massaging his throbbing knee.

While he caught his breath, he pondered the mystery of Vic Maynard. Why would the man gun down the Tattens? John and Lucille had been unarmed and so could not possibly have posed a threat of bodily harm to Maynard and his men. The sheriff had more than a dead youth's scribbled testimony now. The very fact that Maynard was running—and had tried to kill *him*—proved his guilt.

What could have changed the man? Everyone liked him. Even more, he had the utmost respect of everyone in Natrona County for his generous contributions to community projects. As far as Iron knew the man had never had any kind of confrontation with any of his neighbors—or anyone else in the county, for that matter. Never had the sheriff heard a bad word about the man, and neither had he ever—in all the many hours spent in conversation over the years—heard so much as a harsh word from Maynard. In fact, Iron considered him a good friend.

The rancher had apparently been deeply devoted to his late wife and clearly still loved her. His sons and daughters, their mates, and his grandchildren were the subject of nearly every one of Maynard's conversations, and he was extremely proud of them all and bragged about them continually.

How could this nightmare have happened? Why would a man of Vic Maynard's nature suddenly turn into a rabid killer?

And then there were his ranch hands. Leedom, Rippey, Dungan, Ayers, and Kruse, like all the Circle M men, had never caused any trouble in town or anywhere else in the county. They seemed like honest, decent cowpokes. But Tom Quinn had seen the first four soon after Billy Barton was killed, and according to Billy Barton's message, five of Maynard's hands—and he presumed that it had been those five—had watched their boss kill the Tattens and then four of them had given chase to Billy. Obviously, they had run the youth down and brutally murdered him. But how could this be? It was like something had contaminated the well water at the Circle M, transforming all of them into brutal killers. Sort of like Mr. Hyde in that story by Robert Louis Stevenson.

Shaking his head in puzzlement, the sheriff rose to his feet and continued the pursuit. Sucking air through clenched teeth, he once again tried to ignore the pain. He was not getting any better at it.

Vic Maynard was also in pain. Though his chest pains frightened him, he had no choice but to keep climbing rather than stopping to get the rest his tortured body was demanding. It was the only way he could elude Will Iron. Breathing air through a dry throat into burning lungs, the killer recalled the sound of a waterfall that he had heard a while earlier and longed for water. He had wanted to stop and find it so desperately, but knew he dare not take the time. Rolling his tongue around in his mouth, he tried to work up some moisture, but to no avail. Finally he paused, telling himself it could only be for a moment. While trying to satisfy the cry of his lungs for air, he held a hand to his chest and looked around at the rugged country.

Off to his right were broken cliffs of sandstone, backed by conifer-covered plateaus that in turn preceded countless jagged peaks sharply silhouetted against the clear northern sky. To his left, beyond the great heaps of jumbled rocks strewn along the southern edge of the mountain, were more ragged peaks. The lower ones, reaching nine or ten thousand feet, were dense with forest. Maynard knew that the timberline was about eleven thousand feet. There were many bare, jagged peaks that reached those lofty heights above which the trees could not grow and where only the eagles would venture, soaring starkly against the azure sky.

Have to move on, he told himself. His legs felt as if they were made of lead as he forced himself into motion once again. He had taken only a few steps when the shooting pains in his chest forced him to his knees.

Crouching over, clutching at his chest with both hands, Maynard wept in futile rage at his predicament. His heart was about to explode, his lungs were burning up, and his body was dehydrating. His mouth and throat were as dry as a sandpit, and his strength was almost gone. The face of the man who had reduced him to this state flashed into his mind, and he spat out a strangled curse at Will Iron.

Maynard rued the loss of his horse. If that had not happened, he would be long gone on the other side of the mountains, and right now the acclaimed lawman—the famous tracker of outlaws—would be eating his dust . . . and eating crow.

Suddenly the lawman's reputation of prowess in tracking and capturing outlaws and lawbreakers began preying on Maynard, eroding his confidence. He once again pictured himself being hanged on a gallows with his children looking on, the indomitable sheriff of Natrona County there, smiling triumphantly.

That vision gave the killer the impetus to move on. Straining every tired muscle and breathing raggedly, his chest pains now unrelenting, he pushed on.

The sun was setting when Maynard topped a steep incline and found level ground. Wondering how much longer he could go on, he leaned against a lodgepole pine, wheezing and clutching at his chest. He stood there, using the tree for support, and looked across a small meadow at the dense forest opposite. Abruptly, he blinked, then squinted. Amid the trees were a cabin and a small barn, and to one side of the cabin was a corral with two horses in it. Hope came alive within him. Maynard would steal one of the horses and use it to get away from the sheriff.

After catching his breath, the killer circled around the meadow, staying in the shadows of the forest so as not to be seen by the cabin's occupants. As he drew closer to the buildings, he saw just off the corral a large fenced pasture with a small brook running crookedly across it. The brook was dammed up some one hundred feet outside the pasture by a beaver lodge, forming a pond.

Halting a moment behind a tree, Maynard glanced back to where he had first topped the incline. There was no sign of his pursuer. He would be showing up soon, though—and Maynard intended to be gone when he did.

The pains in his chest remained steady as the fugitive sneaked along the blind side of the cabin, his gun drawn. The place was quiet. No one was in sight. Maynard hoped the owners had no dog. If a yapping mutt announced his presence, he would probably have to kill whoever came to investigate. Moving stealthily, he stayed out of view of the cabin's windows and drew up to the barn. He leaned against the rough wall for a moment, massaging his chest and wishing the pains would stop.

Lifting the latch, he swung the large barn door open. The rusty old hinges complained. Another door was open on the far side of the barn, leading to the corral. The two horses stood placidly in the sunlight, one a piebald gelding and the other a bay mare. The piebald was muscular and appeared to be quite strong. He would take the piebald. Then the thought struck him: He could not leave the mare for Iron to use. He would bridle the mare and take her, too. Once he was a safe distance away, he would let her go.

Two saddles hung on one wall of the barn, and there was a place for a third. Two bridles hung next to the saddles. Taking the best-looking saddle and a bridle, the killer moved cautiously outside to the corral. The piebald nickered as he made the approach, but held still while Maynard put on the tack.

Leaving the animal, he returned to the barn and took the other bridle off the wall, then slipped back outside and bridled the mare. Excited at the prospect of finally eluding the persistent sheriff, the fugitive led the horses to the corral gate and was about to open it when a woman's voice pierced the air behind him.

"Hold it right there, buster, or you're a dead man!"

Maynard was so taken by surprise that the words hit him like punches. He slowly turned around to face her and found himself staring into a double-barreled shotgun. Both hammers were cocked. The two ominous bores pointing directly at his face sent an icy chill slithering down his spine.

Behind the shotgun were the weathered face and flinty eyes of a woman in her mid-sixties. Her expression was one of sullen anger.

"Get them hands in the air, buster!" she bellowed.

Her finger was curled tight over both triggers, the knuckle whitening with tension.

Dropping the reins to the bridles, a stunned Maynard obeyed, thrusting his hands over his head. This woman was quite evidently as tough as the country around her, and he had no doubt that she had it in her to blow him into eternity if he made a wrong move.

"Okay, buster," she growled, her voice flat and hard, "who are you, and why are you stealin' my horses?"

Pains were prickling his chest as the woman's eyes drilled into him. His mind was spinning, trying to come up with some story.

"Well, speak up!" she snapped, shoving the black muzzles closer to his face.

Flicking a glance eastward, fearful that the sheriff would show up any second, he stammered, "Will Iron . . . that is, I mean—"

"Will Iron, you say?" Her voice now held a slightly different note.

Maynard's fear-muddled mind had caused him to utter Iron's name by mistake, but suddenly an idea struck him. This woman lived in the high, remote mountains. It was evident she knew the famous sheriff's name, but chances were she had never seen him. It was worth a gamble. Things could not get any worse than they were.

"Uh, I said my name's Will Iron. You've heard of me, perhaps?"

Squinting, she cocked her head and replied, "Yeah. Will Iron's sheriff of Natrona County . . . but I'm not too sure I believe you're him."

"But I am, ma'am," he assured her with a nod, still holding his hands in the air. "Would you mind if I put my hands down, Missus—"

"Name's Millie Calvert, buster," she said tartly. "Tell

you what. Take 'em down long enough to unbuckle your gun belt and let it drop to the ground."

"But, Mrs. Calvert—"

"Do as I say!" she blared, shaking the shotgun at him.

Afraid to do otherwise, Maynard dropped the gun belt at his feet and raised his hands again.

Millie's lips curled into a snarl. "Lawmen don't go around stealin' people's horses, buster! If you're Will Iron, why'd you sneak in here plannin' on makin' off with these animals? Why didn't you come knock on the door and explain your situation? Somethin' happened to your horse, right?"

The stabbing pains in Maynard's chest were making it difficult to hold his arms up. "Yes, ma'am," he replied with a grunt. "Look, if you'd just let me lower my arms, I could give you my explanation. I've been climbing around these mountains for hours, and I'm having some real bad pains in my chest."

The crusty woman looked thoughtful for a moment, then said, "Okay, buster, go on and let 'em down . . . but bear in mind that I've got this shotgun trained right on your head. You move one foot without me tellin' you to, and your body will be hoppin' around like a chicken that just got the ax!"

Sweat beaded on Maynard's brow as his hands fell to his sides. He wanted to sleeve away the moisture but decided he had better leave it. He did not want Millie Calvert to misjudge the move.

"Well?" she snapped. "I'm waitin' to hear your explanation. And, buster, it better be a good one!"

Maynard nodded. Clearing his throat, he said, "Well, I've been trailing a murderer since this morning. Chased him from Casper into these mountains. A ways back he set off a rockslide trying to kill me, but he only succeeded in burying my horse. He took off on his horse, but the animal broke its leg."

Maynard was studying Millie's eyes to see if she believed him. There was no change in her hard glare, and agitation was still written all over her wrinkled face. She remained silent, ready to hear it all.

Continuing, Maynard then explained that he had managed to catch up to his man, and they had ended up in a fistfight down in a gully. He had knocked the fugitive unconscious, handcuffed him, and started dragging him out of the gully when he began to experience pains in his chest. When the pains persisted, he cuffed the killer to a tree and started out, hoping to find a horse somewhere so he could ride it to the nearest doctor. When he spotted Millie's place and saw the two horses, he decided to take them both, one for himself and the other for his prisoner. He would have returned the animals as soon as possible.

Millie Calvert was a tough woman and not easily persuaded. Vic Maynard watched stubbornness settle on her face as she said, "Sounds like cock-and-bull to me. It still don't explain why you didn't come and ask my permission. And if you're the sheriff, where's your badge?"

Maynard felt his face flush. He had not thought about a badge. Thinking fast, he looked down at his chest and replied, "Well, I'll be! It must have torn loose during the fight. I hadn't noticed."

The old woman was clearly still dubious. Holding the shotgun on him steadily, she growled, "I want you to take the gear off them horses and put it back where you found it. When that's done, you and me are gonna sit down on the front porch of the house."

Maynard squinted at her questioningly. "And do what?"

"Wait for Wayne to come home."

"Who's Wayne?"

"My husband, buster. He'll be home about sundown. I still don't believe your story. But I'll let you tell it to Wayne. He can decide what to do with you."

Maynard thought of using his chest pains as a reason that she should let him go, but the fire in her eyes and the jut of her jaw told him it would be useless. With the cocked shotgun trained on him, he removed the tack and returned it to the barn. Millie then picked up his gun belt, marched him to the porch, and made him sit down on the step while she eased onto a wooden chair and held the shotgun on him.

The sun was nearing the tops of the peaks as the fugitive sat watching for Will Iron to show up. If he did, Maynard was doomed.

But the next arrival was a silver-haired man. He came riding across the meadow and hauled up in front of the porch. Wayne Calvert's eyes went from his wife to the stranger and back again. Dismounting, Calvert asked, "What's goin' on, Millie?"

The woman rose to her feet and stepped over near Maynard, whose eyes were glued to the shotgun. The barrels were now pointed at the porch floor, and Millie's trigger finger had relaxed.

Nodding at the fugitive, the old woman finally answered, "I caught him tryin' to steal Corky and Tess. Says he's Sheriff Will Iron from over at Casper and gave me a pip of a story about why he was takin' 'em without askin' my permission. Figured I'd hold him here till you got home. Let you hear the story and decide whether to believe him or not."

A deep frown furrowed Wayne Calvert's brow. His hands on his hips, he said huskily, "Millie, I've seen Sheriff Iron. This ain't him."

Maynard knew he had to act fast. His desperation spurring him on, he moved with remarkable speed and dexterity and grabbed Millie's shotgun from her hands. Aiming it at her head, he blasted away. Millie Calvert's face disappeared, replaced by blood and smoke.

Her husband started to lunge at Maynard, but the killer swung the smoking weapon around and pulled the trigger of the second barrel. The shotgun boomed again, sending its charge into Wayne Calvert's midsection. The elderly man buckled and collapsed to the ground, blood pooling around his body.

Throwing the empty shotgun down, Maynard grabbed his gun belt and strapped it on while heading for the horse Calvert had been riding. Hauling himself into the saddle, he galloped away.

Chapter Seven

Sheriff Will Iron wanted desperately to catch Vic Maynard before dark. As he limped his way up a narrow, steep trail, following sign left by the fugitive, he hoped he was getting closer. He paused on an open plateau and looked around at the rugged terrain while he caught his breath. The setting sun was throwing dark shadows into the maze of canyons visible from where he stood. It would not be long before night fell.

The left knee had swollen even more, shooting pain up his leg into his torso and down into his foot. Steeling himself for even more pain, he pushed on. Soon he entered deep forest and was in heavy timber when he heard the distinct report of a shotgun, followed quickly by another. Halting, he leaned against a tree, trying to determine which direction the sounds had come from.

Deciding the source had been straight ahead, the sheriff picked up his pace. The pain was horrible, but he hurried on. Suddenly the knee buckled, and he fell hard, rolling amid twigs and pine needles. Groaning from the agony the fall inflicted, he struggled to his feet and continued on, certain that somehow Maynard was involved with the shotgun blasts.

Iron had fallen twice more when, just as he spotted a small meadow ahead, a fresh streak of pain burst in his knee, and he collapsed, sprawling facedown on the ground. His head seemed full of cobwebs, and he fought back the wave of nausea that assailed him. Rolling onto his back, he looked up at towering trees outlined against the late-afternoon sky overhead. They seemed to be spinning. The lawman pulled hard for air, trying to keep from passing out.

He lay still for several minutes, clinging to consciousness by a thread. His head was just beginning to clear when he heard hoofbeats coming ever closer. Had Maynard found a horse and circled back to kill him? With an effort he raised his head and saw the indistinct outline of a horse and rider approaching amid the shadows of the trees. He drew his gun and cocked it, waiting until the man came within pistol range. Suddenly the approaching rider's form became clearer. He was young and skinny and wearing Eastern clothes and a derby hat. "Tripp!" he breathed.

The reporter reached his side and slid from the saddle, hunkering down beside the injured lawman. "Sheriff," the reporter whispered anxiously, "are you all right?"

Sitting up and holstering his gun, Iron said through clenched teeth, "Banged my knee up pretty bad. I was almost buried in a rockslide—I think Maynard somehow caused it. Killed my horse."

"I know. I was quite a ways behind you at that time," Tripp said, "but I saw Maynard loosen the rock that set off the slide. I shouted a warning, but it was too late for you to hear me. By the time I arrived at the place where your horse was buried, you were already higher up in pursuit of Maynard. I thought you were under the rubble with your horse till I spotted you up on the side of the mountain. I recognized your hat."

The sheriff looked up at the newcomer and scowled. "What are you doing here, anyway, Mr. Tripp? I told you to stay in town."

The reporter pushed back his derby and scratched

his forehead, replying, "I wanted to get an eyewitness account of your catching and arresting Maynard. You gotta admit, it would add a real strong touch to my article—not to mention to my career."

"But I told you—"

"I know, Sheriff, but look at it this way. Maynard's on foot—I found his dead horse while coming up the trail—but you can ride double with me on my horse, and we'll catch up to him faster."

"Yeah, but I warned you of the danger involved in this chase. I can't have you with me when I catch up to him. You could stop a bullet."

Readjusting his derby, Tripp shrugged. "I'm not worried about that. A good reporter doesn't consider the danger he might encounter while getting a story. He's bent on one thing: getting the story!"

Iron struggled to rise, favoring his bad leg. Tripp took hold of an arm and helped him.

"How did you injure the knee?" the reporter queried.

"Did it when I leapt from my horse to avoid the falling rocks. Smashed it against something. I'm afraid I hurt it pretty bad." Looking westward and changing the subject, Iron said, "I heard a couple of shotgun blasts a few minutes ago. I was hurrying to see what had happened when I fell and almost passed out."

"I heard them myself. Well, let's get aboard the horse and go find out," Tripp said eagerly.

The reporter boosted Iron into the saddle, then hopped up behind him, letting the sheriff have the reins. Iron directed the animal toward the clearing he had been heading for, and moments later they emerged from the deep shadows of the forest into the meadow, which was bathed in the soft light of the setting sun.

Immediately, Iron spotted the cabin amid the trees on the opposite side of the meadow and put the horse to a canter. As they drew near the cabin, they saw the two sprawled bodies, a man in front of the house and a woman lying on the porch. Behind him, Iron heard the reporter gasp.

Iron slid from the saddle and Tripp hopped down after him. "You check the man while I see to the woman," the lawman instructed.

Tripp nodded and rushed to Wayne Calvert.

Iron had gotten one foot on the porch step when he saw the bloody, meaty mass that had been Millie Calvert's face. His stomach lurched. At the same instant Tripp called out that the man was alive. Fighting back the urge to heave, the sheriff limped over to Tripp and the wounded settler.

The lawman took one look at the gaping, bleeding hole in the man's stomach and knew he was mortally wounded.

"How about the woman?" Tripp asked.

Iron shook his head. "She took a shotgun blast in the face," he said softly.

"Oh," Tripp murmured, glancing at the double-barreled shotgun lying in the dust a few feet away.

Calvert's torso and legs were red with his blood, while his face was an alabaster mask. His eyes were closed and he was breathing in short, barely audible gasps. Gently squeezing the settler's shoulder, Iron said, "Sir, my name is Will Iron. I'm the sheriff in the next county. Can you hear me?"

Calvert's glassy eyes fluttered open, and he nodded slowly. His mouth moved wordlessly for a few moments, then he managed to say in a weak voice, "I . . . know who . . . you are. He . . . he killed Millie. Then . . . he turned the gun . . . on me."

"The man who did this—do you know him?" Iron asked, supporting the dying man's head.

Licking his dry lips, Calvert choked out how the killer had tried to convince Millie that he was the lawman and how when Calvert had come back and said the man was an impostor, the man had shot them down.

"Can you describe him, sir?"

Calvert grunted. "Yeah. Heavyset man . . . with silver hair."

Iron and Tripp exchanged glances, nodding to each other. The description confirmed what they had already assumed.

Licking his lips again, Calvert said weakly, "Get him, Sheriff. He . . . killed my wife."

Iron promised, "You can bank on it, sir." He paused, then asked, "What is your name?"

Calvert told him.

The sheriff knew the man would soon be gone. Wanting to make him as comfortable as possible until the end came, he said, "Mr. Calvert, my friend and I will carry you inside and put you on your bed. Will that be all right?"

Calvert nodded slowly. "Thank you."

The two men carried the settler into the cabin, which consisted of one large room with a kitchen area at the far end and a separate bedroom that opened off the back of the cabin and looked as though it had been added on. They took Calvert into the bedroom, which was furnished simply with a bed, a dresser, and a chifforobe, and laid him gently on the bed, then returned to the main room.

Iron looked around the structure as he walked to the kitchen area. A loft—presumably meant for sleeping—had been built into the front end of the cabin, starting just above the front door and running the width of the building to the back wall. The loft was reachable by an attached ladder and had a window that overlooked the front yard. The lawman wondered if the couple had had children and if that was where they had slept. He looked in the kitchen cupboards till he found a glass, then pumped some water into it and brought it to the dying man, who took a few sips, then lay still, his eyes closed and his breathing shallow.

Steeling themselves, the sheriff and his companion brought Millie Calvert's body inside, putting the corpse on the couple's sagging couch and then covering her with a blanket. When Iron and Tripp returned to the back room to look in on Wayne Calvert, the last glimmer of daylight showed on the jagged peaks visible from the bedroom window, and the settler was dead.

They carried the old woman's body to the bedroom and placed her beside her husband. Then the travelers returned to the kitchen and sat down at the table.

"Well," Iron sighed, lighting a lamp against the gathering gloom, "it looks like the chase will go on tomorrow."

"He's gonna get a good start on us since he's got a horse," Tripp noted.

"Us?" Iron repeated, arching his eyebrows. "I think not."

"Aw, come on, Sheriff," the reporter protested. "I want to go with you."

"Nope. I noticed two horses out there in the corral. One of them's a big piebald. I'll take him and go after Maynard at first light. I want you to stay here and bury the Calverts."

Tripp glowered but remained silent.

"Anyway, I don't think Maynard's going to have gotten too far," the lawman mused. "He hadn't been gone very long when we showed up, and I doubt he'd be riding in this rugged country at night—unless he's a bigger fool than I think he is. Too many crevices and canyons to fall into. I'll get him tomorrow."

The two men settled in for the night, preparing supper together. While they ate, the reporter made another attempt at getting the obdurate lawman to change his mind. "Tell you what, Sheriff," Tripp said casually.

"There's a good moon out there tonight. I'll bury the Calverts now so I can ride with you in the morning."

Will Iron grinned and shook his head. "You're a persistent cuss, aren't you?"

"It takes persistence to make it as a reporter."

"You're not going with me, Bernie. Do your burying when you want, but you're staying here in the morning."

Tripp fixed him with a level stare. "You're a stubborn cuss, aren't you?"

There was a twinkle in Iron's eye as he retorted, "It takes stubbornness to make it as a lawman."

Tripp ran a palm over his face. "So I'm to stay here till when?" he asked in a resigned voice.

"Till I come back with my prisoner. I promise you this: No matter where I capture him, I'll come back here. We'll ride to Casper together . . . you, me, and Vic Maynard." Iron paused, took a sip of coffee, then said, "If you want an eyewitness experience to write about, stick around a few days after we get back to Casper, and you can watch Maynard hang. That'll make an interesting firsthand story."

After eating, the two men washed the dishes and utensils. When they were finished, Iron decided to check the loft, to see if there were any mattresses up there. Turning from the sink, he gasped as pain tore through his left leg. His knee gave way, and he slipped, keeping himself from falling only by grabbing the edge of the counter.

Tripp helped him over to a chair. "I'll check the loft, Sheriff. You rest that knee."

"Think I'd better soak it in hot water," Iron commented. "How about heating up some water for me?"

When the water was heated and poured into a big, galvanized tub, the sheriff removed his boot, rolled up his pants leg, and sat with his leg partly submerged. The knee was an angry red, and swollen to nearly twice its normal size. While Iron tried soothing his injury with a hot compress, using the dish towel, Tripp climbed to the loft and found two old horsehair mattresses lying on the floor, along with pillows and blankets.

"How about if I bring down one of those mattresses for you, Sheriff?" the reporter asked after coming back down and announcing his find. But Iron insisted he could make the climb.

While Iron continued to minister to his knee, the young reporter sat at the table, making notes for his article. Laying down his pencil, Tripp looked over at the lawman and smiled. "Tell you what, Sheriff. Even if you won't let me be in on Maynard's capture, this is turning out to be quite a story."

Vic Maynard had pushed Wayne Calvert's horse west toward the timberline, planning to find a natural mountain pass, descend, and head north. When the day came that he felt enough time had elapsed for Will Iron to give up the chase—and maybe even give up the law—and for any wanted poster put out on him to be long forgotten, he would be able to return to Wyoming. Of course, by then maybe it would not even matter. If in the intervening period he had persuaded his family to join him up in Canada, there would be nothing to return to.

He had picked his way across the mountain in the fading light, and when it got too dark to safely negotiate the crevices and cliffs, the killer hauled up in a rocky area beneath towering pines, their tops rustling from the wind. When the sun dropped, so did the temperature, and Maynard knew he would have to find a shelter from the wind to spend the night. In the thick twilight he spotted a rock overhang at the base of a massive boulder. From what he could make out he would be able to crawl in about six feet beneath the overhang and at least get out of the wind.

As Maynard tied the horse to a slender tree, his stomach growled, hunger gnawing at his innards, and he berated himself for not having taken the time to grab some food from the Calverts' kitchen. He checked Wayne Calvert's saddlebags, hoping the settler had been carrying some food, but they were empty. Picturing Will Iron finding the Calverts' bodies, Maynard cursed the lawman, hating the man for his relentless pursuit.

He would have to pull out at first light and keep moving fast if he was going to make it to freedom. That meant not even stopping to hunt for a rabbit—much less take the time to skin and cook it. The thought of food and water tormented Maynard as he sat down on a fallen log and watched the stars come out in the black-velvet sky overhead. Soon the moon lifted over the peaks, silhouetting the swaying trees overhead. The branches reminded him of a gallows and of the fact that Iron was dogging his tracks to end his life with a hangman's noose. A cold shiver went through him.

Exhausted and doing his best to ignore his terrible hunger and thirst, Maynard stood up and walked the few steps to the overhang. Dropping to his knees, he crawled back as far as he could go, removed his hat to use it as a pillow, and stretched out. The earth was soft beneath the rock shelf, and it felt good to lie down. The pains in his chest were only intermittent now and less severe. Having the horse to ride had made a real difference.

The wind that whined over the mountain and whistled continuously through the treetops soon lulled the fugitive to sleep.

A wolf howled somewhere nearby, and the killer jerked awake, cracking his head on the stone only inches above him. Cursing silently while rubbing his head, he looked out at the horse, which was whinnying nervously and dancing about.

Maynard pulled his revolver and tensed, waiting to

see if the horse would settle down. It finally did. It nickered lightly, and then all was quiet except the wind. Gripping the gun, the killer lay back down. His mind went to his family in Nebraska. He missed his children; even more, he missed his grandchildren. Would they grow up without him being able to see it happen?

Memories of times with his family flooded his mind. He ached to see them. He thought of Martha and felt the emptiness that her death had left in his heart. When his mind drifted back to his offspring, he gritted his teeth and vowed that they would never know what he had been and what he had become. Exhausted, his body finally relaxed and he was able to go back to sleep.

It was sometime in the middle of the night when Maynard was again awakened suddenly. Opening his eyes, he listened intently. Then, over the sound of the wind rushing through the treetops, a wolf gave a long, mournful howl, much closer than before. Maynard gasped at a sudden cold sensation, as if an icicle had pierced his chest. The horse was whinnying and prancing fearfully.

Gripping his gun, Maynard crawled outside. The wind plucked at his thinning hair as he slowly and carefully paced the area, holding the gun ready while trying to peer into the dappled shadows. He knew by the horse's fear that the wolf was lurking near, but he saw nothing. Going to the horse, he stroked its long neck and said soothingly, "It's okay, boy. If that critter shows up, I'll put a bullet in its heart."

Maynard kept talking to the frightened animal while studying the shadows. After several minutes the horse settled down again and, shivering with cold, Maynard returned to his makeshift shelter.

Keeping the revolver in hand, the fugitive lay awake for a long time, listening for the horse to show further signs of nervousness. The wind continued to moan over the rocks, emphasizing the loneliness that Vic Maynard was feeling. He thought about his men and how they had betrayed him and how he would somehow get revenge. If they had remained true to him, he would not be out in these mountains with Will Iron breathing down his neck. Leedom and the others would live to rue the day they set him up to fall into the hands of the law.

The exhausted fugitive was almost asleep again when he was startled by a shrill scream from the horse. The scream was still echoing in the air when it was punctuated by snarling and growling. Shaking his head to clear it, Maynard crawled over onto his belly and stared out with horror at what he saw illuminated so clearly by the moonlight: A pack of ravenous wolves was attacking the defenseless horse, snapping at its throat and tearing its flesh. The poor animal was shrieking in terror, struggling to break free from the reins that held it fast to the tree.

Swearing, Maynard took aim at one of the wolves. There were so many that it was hard to get off a clear shot without the risk of hitting the horse.

Maynard's gun roared. The wolf he had sighted in on went down with a yelp and lay still, but the biggest one in the pack had opened the horse's throat with a violent slash of razor-sharp fangs. The horse kicked and screamed, trying to fight off its attackers. One of the pack took a hoof in the side and rolled several feet. Gritting his teeth, Maynard fired again, putting a bullet through the head of a second wolf.

The other attackers looked toward the source of the muzzle flash, then darted for cover. Maynard fired after them in a frenzy for having robbed him of his mount. Now he would be afoot again. Blinded by fury, Maynard kept pulling the trigger long after the gun was empty.

When the horse keeled over and hit the ground with a loud "whump," the crazed fugitive came to his senses and finally realized he was out of ammunition. Cautiously, he crawled out from under the rock overhang, holding the gun as if it were still useful. He glanced at the two wolves he had shot; they lay still in death. Movement from beyond the fallen horse drew his attention to the wolf that had taken the violent kick in the side. It was still alive, lying in a spot where the moon shone directly on it. The beast lay watching the man's movements warily, panting shallowly from fear and pain. Maynard had seen the wolf take the severe blow and assumed by the way its side was caved in that all the ribs on that side had been broken.

Hating the animal for destroying his transportation, Maynard approached it, saying venomously, "Got yourself hurt pretty bad, didn't you? Can't move, eh? Too bad, 'cause I'm gonna kill you."

Even as he spoke, Maynard circled around behind the wolf while turning the revolver in his hand to use it as a club. The animal snarled and snapped at him, rolling its head back, but it was unable to rise. Swearing furiously at the wolf, the killer bent and slammed the gun against the animal's head. The beast yelped and snapped weakly at its attacker. Maynard brought the weapon down again, smashing the skull with all his strength. The wolf went limp and breathed its last.

Kicking the dead wolf, Maynard shoved the empty gun in its holster and stepped to the horse, which lay on its side, breathing hard and nickering quietly. Its ears were laid back and its eyes were bulging. Blood was pumping fast from the slash in its throat, pooling under the long neck.

Maynard felt waves of despair wash over him, and heaviness descended like a tangible weight. Alternately swearing and moaning and stamping his feet, he cursed his rotten luck. He was on foot again, and Iron would no doubt be on one of Calvert's horses. The exertion would surely bring on more chest pains, and Maynard feared his heart would give out. The more he contemplated his predicament, the more the heaviness pressed down on him. Pressure began to build inside his head, and his neck and back muscles stiffened. His breathing came in short gasps, and cold sweat beaded his brow, chilled by the wind so that it felt like little particles of ice.

He was in a terrible bind. If he stayed where he was and Iron caught him, he would die at the end of a rope. If he pushed himself too hard in his desperate bid for freedom, he could die of heart failure. Maynard did not like either option, but at least he had some chance that his heart would not give out. He had no chance of beating the hangman. His only hope was to stay on the move. Maybe he would find another cabin soon. If he could get his hands on another horse, he still had a chance of escaping Iron. And if he could come by some cartridges that fit his gun—or even pick up another gun—he could still make it.

A wolf howled somewhere higher up the mountain. Seconds later, another wolf howled in return. Maynard swore at them, hoping he would not meet up with them again. He looked eastward, noting that the stars were already fading in the predawn light.

He waited another quarter hour, when dawn began to illuminate the dangerous crevices on the steep mountainside. Steeling himself, he began climbing higher, casting a long look behind him and surveying the rugged mountain. Will Iron was down there somewhere, probably riding after him at that very moment. Pain suddenly stabbed into Maynard's chest, but he pushed on, panic picking at his brain.

Chapter Eight

Sheriff Will Iron awakened from his sound sleep, and for a moment he did not know where he was. Then he remembered he was in the Calverts' cabin, and he sat up and looked out the loft window onto a new dawn. Slipping off the mattress, he crawled past Bernie Tripp, who was quietly snoring, and eased his way down the ladder. There was no time to make breakfast, but he found some hardtack on top of the cupboard.

Grabbing a handful, he stuck a piece in his mouth, put the open canister back where he had found it, and limped outside. Quietly, he closed the door, went to the barn, and quickly saddled the piebald, then rode out in pursuit of Vic Maynard.

The sun was up but had not yet appeared above the towering peaks to the east as Will Iron picked up Maynard's trail and put the piebald to a trot. As he rode under the flawless sky, it seemed to him as though the wind was picking up again. It did not take long for Iron to near the spot where Maynard had spent the night. As he rounded the massive boulder where the rock overhang was situated, he jerked back on the reins at the sight of the dead horse and wolves.

Noticing the deep recess, the sheriff immediately theorized that Maynard had spent the night in its shelter and wondered if the killer might still be there. He dismounted and inched his way toward the front of the overhang, revolver drawn and ready, then bent over and looked under the shelf. It was empty.

Since the fugitive had not been too far ahead of the lawman the evening before, Iron assumed that he had gotten only this far when darkness fell and had hauled up here for the night. No doubt the wolves had attacked the horse sometime during the night, and Maynard had struck out on foot at first light.

Iron moved carefully about, studying the ground. It took only a couple of minutes to pick up Maynard's trail. The fugitive was continuing toward the timberline, apparently planning to reach the other side of the mountain and make his escape. Limping back to the piebald, the lawman struggled into the saddle, dismayed that the swelling, which had gone down a bit while he slept, had almost immediately returned once he had put his weight back on the knee. Well, he would quickly overtake Maynard now, since the man was on foot. Guiding his mount around the boulder, Iron put the animal to a trot again.

Maynard's trail was easy to follow, and Iron's seasoned eye told him that the footprints in the soft earth were only minutes old. The lawman was nearing an open area in his climb when he heard a cascade of small rocks. Slowing the piebald, he looked up to see Vic Maynard scurrying higher. The killer was nearing the timberline, attempting to make his way up a steep, rocky path amid a thin stand of stunted pines.

Iron put the horse to a canter, then reined in sharply when they reached the base of the path. There was no way the piebald could climb it. He winced when he dismounted, but having his man in sight was enough to spur him on, and he began climbing the nearly vertical slope with vigor.

*   *   *

Two hundred feet above, Vic Maynard was experiencing severe chest pains as he clawed his way toward the top of the mountain. His lungs seemed aflame, and his throat was begging for moisture, but he pushed on, telling himself he could rest a bit once he was over the top.

At that point he happened to look over his shoulder and, to his horror, saw that his pursuer had again caught up with him and was at that moment starting up after him. "No!" he gasped, panic rising within him. Expending himself to the limit, Maynard picked up his pace. The haunting vision of his execution, his children standing below the gallows, flashed into his mind once more, and fear-inspired frenzy made him climb even faster. Each jolt of pain that lanced his chest made him flinch, and he whimpered in agony.

When the killer was only a few feet from the top, he looked back to see Iron gaining on him. Hatred of the lawman boiled his blood and gave him renewed strength. His breath wheezed in and out as he cursed Iron and kept climbing.

Crumpled rock and loose shale made it difficult to rise steadily. For every three or four steps, he slipped back two. He prayed for relief, but none could be had—other than eluding Iron . . . and the hangman's noose. Grasping the jagged outcroppings had turned his hands raw and bloody, but he kept moving upward, stark panic driving him on.

At last Maynard was within a few feet of the top. He had to find a hiding place fast, as soon as he was out of Iron's sight. Straining every muscle, he lunged upward and bellied over the craggy crest. A flat granite shelf lay some ten feet below him, and, letting go, he slid down to it on his belly, landing hard. Breathing raggedly, he rose to his feet to flee when he realized he was standing on the ledge of a deep canyon. He was at a dead end.

He had no way to go but back the way he had come. Inching his way to the lip of the flat surface, he peered down into the abyss. Its bottom was so far below that it was buried in dark, fathomless shadows.

A fierce wind whipped up out of the canyon, almost throwing him off balance. As he staggered back from the edge, the wind plucked his hat from his head and sent it soaring into space.

Pivoting, Maynard looked back at the crest he had just topped. He could hear Will Iron coming. Terror seared his brain like a hot knife. There was nowhere to run.

The lawman's adrenaline was surging, filling his body with energy as he scaled the steep path, closing in on the fugitive. The anticipation of finally capturing his man blocked the pain in his knee from his mind. With his attention so focused on his objective, he was unaware that Bernie Tripp had disobeyed his orders once more and was coming up behind him.

The chase was almost over. Iron all but had Maynard in his grasp. The killer had just disappeared over the top of the mountain some seventy feet above him. Iron scurried up to the crest and peered over it. He expected to see the fugitive picking his way down the mountain as quickly as he could in a desperate bid to escape. What he found instead was Vic Maynard staring up at him, his face white and his body trembling as he stood six feet away from the lip of a canyon, the wind whipping his clothing and his hair.

Maynard was clearly in a frenzy as Iron topped the rocky path, blocking the only escape route. Holding his gun on the killer, Iron demanded, "Drop your gun belt."

Maynard licked his cracked lips and eyed the lawman

with hate-filled eyes. "The gun's empty. I used the last slugs to shoot at the wolves that took down my horse."

"Drop it anyway," Iron growled.

"You're not taking me in," Maynard warned. He glanced over his shoulder at the edge of the canyon just feet away. "I'm not going to give my men the satisfaction of seeing me paraded through town in chains. Not after they double-crossed me and turned me in."

"Turned . . . ? What are you talking about?"

"It was Leedom and the others, wasn't it?"

Iron peered at him, bewildered. "You ought to know. You gave the order for them to murder Billy."

A gust of wind suddenly howled up out of the canyon, and Maynard had to shout to be heard. "You mean they *did* kill the kid?" he asked, his face filled with confusion.

"Yeah, and they'll hang for it, too. Now, I'll say it again, Vic: Drop the gun belt."

Maynard looked stunned. Ignoring the demand, he asked, "If my men didn't turn me in, then . . . then how did you find out?"

"That you murdered the Tattens?"

"Yeah."

"Billy told me."

Maynard stared at the lawman. "I thought you said that Billy's dead."

"Oh, he's dead, all right. But he was a bright young man. He scratched a message in Tom Quinn's barn saying what had happened and who did it." Iron's voice turned colder as he added, "He also said that your men were trying to kill him because he witnessed you murdering the Tattens."

Maynard's eyes were wild.

Would the rancher leap to his death rather than face a rope? Wanting to calm him down, Iron asked, "Tell me, Vic, why *did* you murder John and Lucille? None of this makes any sense to me. I've known you for four years now, and I've always admired you, respected you . . . *liked* you. You've been my friend, and I know you well—or I thought I knew you well. What happened?"

The wild look in Maynard's eyes was replaced by hatred. "Because they were blackmailing me."

"I don't understand," Iron responded.

Maynard told Iron of his past and that he had been able to keep it from his wife and children . . . until John Tatten had somehow found out and blackmailed him. "I paid him ten thousand. Ten thousand!" he repeated. "But the Tattens weren't satisfied with that— Lucille especially. They wanted more. And after that they'd have probably wanted more still. My only way out was to kill them." He looked deeply into Iron's eyes, as if asking for his forgiveness. "I'm sorry that Billy Barton got caught up in the whole thing. Nobody innocent was supposed to get hurt."

Iron shook his head angrily. "Why didn't you just come to me and tell me what the Tattens were doing, Vic? Blackmailing's against the law. I could have helped you."

"What, and take a chance on my kids finding out that their father's an ex-convict? I couldn't let that happen."

"They're going to find out anyway. I have to take you in. You must face trial and hang."

"*No!*" Maynard screamed over the howling wind. "I can't let that happen! The only thing I have left in the world is the love and respect of my sons and daughters and their families. Everything they ever felt for me would be wiped out by a trial. I can't let that happen! I can't go to my grave knowing that they despise me! I can't let them learn of this!"

Iron knew Maynard was thinking of jumping into the canyon. "Your children will learn of it anyhow, Vic!" he shouted. "Everybody will! When I return, I'll have to make a report on the Tattens' killer!"

Maynard's head snapped back and forth. Tears spilled from his eyes and were quickly whipped away by the wind. Wailing with anguish, he cried, "I can't face my children, Will!" As he cried, he wheeled and leapt over the edge.

Will Iron scrambled down to the ledge and looked into the canyon. Vic Maynard plummeted silently into the black chasm; within seconds, he was out of sight.

The sheriff turned away, shaking his head. He stopped suddenly when he found Bernie Tripp standing in front of him.

"Wow, what a story!" the reporter exclaimed. "I can see the headline now: SHERIFF WILL IRON HUNTS DOWN KILLER LIKE MAD DOG . . . KILLER TAKES COWARD'S WAY OUT!"

Iron regarded Tripp coldly. "A man has met a horrible, tragic end. Doesn't that matter? You newspeople, you have to sensationalize everything, don't you?"

The reproachful words clearly stung, but Tripp airily responded, "It's the way we make our living, Sheriff."

Iron sighed. He glanced back briefly at the canyon, then remarked, "Well, there's no way we can retrieve Maynard's body. Let's head back for Casper."

Tripp looked away for a moment, then said sheepishly, "We'll, uh, we'll need to stop at the cabin and bury the Calverts first."

The lawman fixed him with a cold stare. "That's what I left you there to do."

"I realize that. But I knew if I followed you, I'd get a jim-dandy story." He grinned. "And now I've got it!"

Iron knew that further remonstration was pointless. After all, as the reporter had already pointed out, he was just being as dogged in his profession as the lawman was in his.

The two men returned to the cabin and buried the Calverts. They spent the night there, giving Iron's knee a much-needed rest, then rode out at dawn. Not wanting to impede their progress, the lawman decided to leave the Calverts' bay mare behind, since there was plenty of water and pasture for the animal. A letter he had found in the cabin from a friend of the Calverts in Lander, Wyoming, gave him someone to contact regarding next of kin, if any, and disposition of the Calverts' horses and property.

It was late evening by the time the two riders rode into Casper. Iron's knee had gotten worse than ever, and the swelling had extended down his leg. The lawman told the reporter, "I'm going straight to Doc Boulder's office. Do me a favor, would you? Before you go to your hotel room, would you ride to my house and tell my wife where I am and why?"

"Sure," Tripp agreed. "Just tell me where your house is."

Iron directed him, then headed toward the infirmary, which was at the southern end of Main Street. Reaching the clinic, he looked up and saw lights shining brightly in the doctor's residence above the office. He was glad he would not be disturbing Joel and Martha Boulder, although he knew the physician and his wife were used to such intrusions. Dismounting, he limped to the front door and knocked. Moments later a lamp was lit at the bottom of the stairs, and then the curtain on the front door was parted, displaying Dr. Boulder's face. The door swung open, and the doctor, a handsome man in his early forties, smoothed back his thick, slightly ruffled black hair and smiled. "Howdy, Will. Glad you're back. Catch Maynard?"

"In a sense I did," Iron replied. "He's dead. Took his own life by jumping over a cliff so he wouldn't have to hang. I hurt my left knee pretty bad while pursuing him. Can you take a look at it?"

"Certainly. Come on in."

Boulder sat the sheriff down and examined the knee. Frowning, he stated, "You've cracked your kneecap, Will. It's filled with fluid that'll have to be drained, and then I'm going to have to perform some surgery and see if I can close up the crack. If I don't, you'll lose the use of the knee altogether."

The news was not what Iron had been hoping to hear, but he knew the doctor would do what was best for him. "I understand. Let's get started."

Iron was stretched out on the examining table and Boulder was draining fluid with a long needle when a knock sounded at the infirmary door.

"That'll probably be Vanessa," Iron said. "I had someone go tell her I'd be here."

Boulder called for the sheriff's wife to come in. The redhead entered, Bernie Tripp on her heels, and rushed across the room with worry written on her face. Taking her husband's hand, she gasped, "Will, Mr. Tripp told me what happened! Thank heaven you weren't buried in that rockslide!"

Iron grinned. "I told you before I left that I had too much waiting at home for me not to come back." Squeezing her hand, he assured her, "Don't worry. Doc's going to fix me up like new."

Boulder shook his head and said, "I don't know about that, Will."

"What do you mean, Doctor?" Vanessa asked, concern furrowing her brow.

"I mean it may bother that knee if he puts any strain on it."

"Will it affect his work as a lawman?"

"That depends," replied the physician. "If he chases

any more criminals into the mountains, then, yes, definitely it'd affect it."

"Good thing that only happens once in a while," Iron quipped.

Boulder raised his eyes. "Once in a while is all it'd take." He looked at Vanessa and told her, "It's time to go to work on that kneecap. You can wait in the outer office or stay in here. Whichever you prefer."

"I'll stay in here," she replied quickly, still gripping her husband's hand.

Nodding, the physician turned to the reporter. "Mr. Tripp, I'll have to ask you to wait outside till surgery's completed."

Tripp shook his head and stepped up beside the table. "No, that won't be necessary. Sheriff, I'll say good-bye now. I found out there's a train coming through first thing in the morning, heading east, and I'm going to be on it. I'm anxious to get back and write my article about you. With what you told me about yourself and what I saw with my own eyes, I've really got quite a story to write." Extending his hand, he gripped Iron's. "Thanks for putting up with me."

The lawman grinned. "Thanks for helping me out when I needed you . . . even if you did disobey a few orders."

As soon as Bernie Tripp had bid Vanessa good-bye and left, the physician administered ether to his patient to begin the surgery. From across the room Vanessa asked, "When can I take him home, Doctor?"

"Not until morning," Boulder replied. "Anytime after eight."

The redhead nodded. "Okay. I'll come for him in a carriage at eight."

Boulder glanced over at her and smiled reassuringly. "Don't worry about your husband. He'll be fine. He's tough. It'll take a lot more than a banged-up knee to get him down."

"I know," Vanessa agreed, sighing. "That's one of the many reasons I love him."

It was almost noon the next day when, at the Circle M Ranch, Carl Leedom, Lou Rippey, J. P. Ayers, and Dean Dungan were sitting on the porch of the big ranch house, wondering about Vic Maynard.

"I guess there's nothin' we can do but wait till we hear somethin'," Ayers said.

Dean Dungan suddenly straightened in his chair and pointed with his chin, saying, "Oh, oh. Maybe we got trouble, fellas."

The others looked over to see Deputy Jim Stenzel riding in, leading a dozen men on horseback.

"Do you suppose Iron caught Vic and has sent a posse after us?" Dungan asked.

"I don't know," Leedom put in, rising to his feet. "Seems to me Iron would come himself if that's what it was. Everybody just remain calm. There's no way the law can know it was us who killed the Barton kid—unless Vic told on us. And you know that ain't gonna happen. Let's see what Stenzel's got on his mind."

The others stood as well and stepped to the edge of the porch as Stenzel and his posse drew up. Each of the riders wore a sidearm and was holding a rifle or a shotgun. Some of the other Circle M men were wandering over from the corral, obviously curious, but Leedom waved them off. Pulling a cigarillo from a shirt pocket, he stuck it in the corner of his mouth and said lightly, "What's this, Deputy? You fellas look like you're ready for a war."

Dismounting, Stenzel stepped up to the porch and replied, "All depends on you and your cohorts."

Leedom squinted down at him, pulled out a match,

and struck it with his thumbnail. Lighting up, he took a drag and, the cigarillo dangling from a corner of his mouth, said, "I don't get your meanin', Deputy."

The possemen slid from their saddles and spread out in front of the porch. The four men on the porch tensed.

Stenzel tipped his hat to the back of his head, ran his gaze over each of the killers' faces, and said levelly, "You're all under arrest for the murder of Billy Barton. You can drop your gun belts and come quietly, or you can make a battle out of it. I think you're smart enough to see that if you try to resist arrest, you'll die where you stand."

Fear showed on the three underlings' faces, while Leedom's displayed anger. But before he could speak, Stenzel demanded, "Where's Ed Kruse?"

"Ridin' fence," Leedom grunted. "Where do you get off comin' out here and arrestin' us for somethin' we didn't do?"

"We've got it on solid word that you four chased Billy down and killed him and that you and Ed Kruse were with Vic Maynard and stood idly by while Maynard gunned down John and Lucille Tatten. Kruse will face charges of being an accessory to the Tattens' murder, but you boys will be tried for murdering Billy. Believe me, it'll stick. You're going to hang."

Carl Leedom's face darkened dangerously. "You're bluffin'!" he spat.

The possemen brought their weapons into ready position. Stenzel's cold stare bore into Leedom. "This is no bluff. Vic Maynard himself confessed to Sheriff Iron before he committed suicide—and Billy inscribed a message on the lid of Tom Quinn's feed bin, telling everything."

The words hit the four men like so many bullets, and they stood rigid, eyes wide and mouths gaping.

"You heard me right," the deputy assured them. "Your boss is dead. Said he couldn't face his children, then took a leap into the canyon that Sheriff Iron had cornered him in."

Leedom's cigarillo fell from his mouth to the porch floor as he blurted, "You can't hang us! Nobody witnessed anything!"

"Oh, you'll hang, all right!" Stenzel promised. "Between Billy's message and the sheriff's testimony attesting to Maynard's confession, there's more than enough evidence. Now, drop your gun belts!"

Will Iron attended the trial three days later on crutches. He was satisfied that justice had been served when the judge sentenced Billy Barton's killers to hang the next day, while Ed Kruse was given twenty years in Wyoming State Penitentiary.

After the hangings, Iron was returning to his office with Vanessa and Jim Stenzel when council chairman Ty Miller, who was leading a delegation of officials, approached him and said, "Will, the county authorities want to talk to you. Would now be a good time to meet?"

"Certainly," the lawman replied.

Together the Irons, the deputy, and the officials went to the sheriff's office. Iron took his seat behind his desk while Vanessa stood beside him.

Miller got right to the point. "Will, to be frank, we're concerned that your knee will hinder you from doing your job."

The sheriff shook his head. "I can understand why you gentlemen would be concerned, but Doc Boulder says I'll be okay. I'm healing fast, and I'll be as good as new in no time."

Vanessa put her hand on her husband's. "Will, I haven't said anything, but I share the concern of these good men. Dr. Boulder did say the knee may never be the same, that it could bother you if you put a strain on it. And in your work, there are times when that won't be avoidable. I really think you should consider retiring. You're such a resourceful man. I know you'll find a way to earn a living that won't endanger your life because of a bad knee."

Iron patted his wife's hand. "Honey, I'll be all right. Don't you worry."

Jim Stenzel took a step closer. "Will, to tell you the truth, your injury has me worried, too. I'd rather see you retire than face some determined gunslick and have your draw slowed because of the knee."

Iron rose to his feet, put the crutches under his arms, and hobbled around his desk to his deputy. Smiling, he slapped the younger man on the back, and said, "I'll be all right, Jim . . . but I'll tell you this: When I *do* retire, I want you to be the man who inherits my badge."

Chapter Nine

Five weeks had passed. During that time, Will Iron, recalling the whereabouts of Vic Maynard's children from numerous conversations the two friends had had over the years, had notified Maynard's oldest son, Vance, of his father's demise. Iron had felt it would serve no purpose to reveal the true circumstances of the rancher's death to Vance: that his father, acting out of a desperate desire to shelter his children from his past, had murdered four people and was responsible for the death of a fifth. Vic Maynard had already paid the ultimate price for his crimes. The lawman thought it wholly unnecessary to destroy the Maynard children's memories of their father.

Out of past friendship and respect for the kind, generous man that Maynard had been until his desperation made him snap, Iron told Vance only that his father had died accidentally while in the mountains and that his body was unrecoverable. Vance wrote back, thanking Iron for letting him know and asking if the lawman would hire a local attorney to handle the sale of the ranch. The lawyer could take his fee from the proceeds when the Circle M was sold and wire on the rest. Iron assured Vance he would take care of it.

It was now early in the third week of May, and Will Iron was back on the job, though he walked with a decided limp. The local newspaper had reported the sheriff's knee injury, and other newspapers had picked up the story about the famous lawman, spreading word of the injury all over Wyoming.

The lawman was out of town, settling a dispute between two local ranchers, when three tough-looking riders rode into Casper. The leader of the bunch, Hank Owens, was a cocky gunslick who had read of Iron's leg injury. Figuring that a bad knee would slow down the famous sheriff's draw, he came to challenge Iron.

"Well, boys," he said to his two companions, his younger brother, Junior, and Mickey Swafford, "I do believe that before this day is over, I'll have the kind of fame that most gunfighters only dream about."

Junior, a hard-faced man in his mid-twenties, chuckled and said, "As your brother, it'd sure make me right proud. And the man who takes down Will Iron will have his name written up in the history books for certain."

Swafford shook his head doubtfully. "Even though Iron's no longer in his prime and has a bad leg?"

"Yeah," Hank replied. "A man of Iron's reputation, it don't matter none that he's old and ailing. Dead is dead."

The trio hauled up and dismounted across the street from the sheriff's office. The older Owens sauntered into the middle of the street, while Junior went into the office to tell Iron he had a challenger outside. But Junior reappeared a few moments later, alone.

"The deputy said Iron's out of town, but he's expected back soon."

"Did you tell him why we're lookin' for his boss?" Hank asked.

Junior grinned. "Nah. I thought I'd let you tell Iron that yourself when he returns."

"What do we do in the meantime?" Swafford queried.

Hank shrugged. "Wait. Let's take a seat on that bench across the street. That way we can watch for him."

Just over an hour later, the sheriff rode in. As he dismounted in front of his office, Hank stepped into the street.

"Iron!" he shouted, his tone challenging. "Your time has come!"

Stiffening, the lawman turned and located the speaker. It was immediately apparent that the man was a gun-fighter, but the lawman asked, "What can I do for you?"

The gunslick grinned. "You mean you ain't figured it out?"

"Oh, I figured it out," Iron said in a long-suffering voice. "Just one look at you told me what it is you want. But I was hoping you'd be smart and change your mind."

Hank chuckled maliciously. "You mean you're hoping I'll be *kind* and change my mind. Take pity on an old cripple."

Not wanting to kill the gunfighter, the lawman ignored the barbs and tried to talk the man out of a contest. "I may be a good ways older than you and have a bad knee, but believe me, I can still outdraw the likes of you. Now, do yourself a favor and get back on your horse and ride out of here . . . while you still can."

Hank turned to his cronies. "You hear that, fellas? The sheriff thinks he can scare me outta takin' him on." He turned back to Iron. "Not a chance, lawman. I've waited a long time for this—and I ain't gonna quit now."

By now a sizable crowd had gathered. Drawn by the commotion outside, Jim Stenzel came out of the office and quickly sized up the situation. "Will, do you want me to help you run these fools out of town?"

Iron shook his head. "It's okay, Jim. I can handle it."
It was obvious to Iron that no amount of cajoling would
alter the gunslick from his course. Shrugging, the sheriff muttered, "He's gonna have to find out the hard way
that he's made a big mistake." He then walked to the
middle of the street, his step determined.

The two men stood facing each other, forty feet apart.
"It's your move, fella," Iron called. "You're the one
who wanted this."

Sneering, Hank went for his gun.

As Iron started to draw his knee gave way and he fell.
The gunslick's bullet barely missed him as he went
down. Hank cocked the trigger to fire again, determined to kill the famous sheriff, but Jim Stenzel fired
first, putting a bullet through the shooter's heart.

The deputy immediately lined his weapon on the
gunfighter's cohorts, warning, "Try anything and you'll
be as dead as your friend."

Though cursing Stenzel for interfering, neither Swafford
nor Junior Owens went for their guns.

Iron was quickly back on his feet and ready for action. Staring at the twosome, his eyes narrowing, the
sheriff told them, "Get out of town and take your dead
pal with you. I don't even want his bones rotting in our
cemetery."

Swafford and Owens struggled to get Hank's body
draped over his horse. Their grim task completed, they
mounted up, and as they did so, Owens said loudly,
"That weren't no fair fight! That deputy had no right to
interfere with the gunfight. He as good as murdered
my brother!"

He glared at Stenzel as they rode out of Casper,
mumbling to Swafford, "We're comin' back. I'm gonna
kill that deputy!"

Iron watched them leave, then limped to the doctor's
office to have Dr. Boulder look at his knee. Vanessa,

having heard of the incident, showed up at the clinic minutes after her husband's arrival, tears in her eyes and concern on her face. "Oh, Will! I heard about your knee giving in and you almost getting yourself killed! Please, I'm begging you! You've got to retire before you leave me a widow and the children without a father!" She began to weep, and her tears cut Will Iron to the quick.

Taking his wife's hand, Iron tried to reason with her. "I'll be all right, darlin'. I'm just too young to retire. This was just an isolated incident. Doc says I've just strained the tendons. He'll wrap it good, and it'll heal again in no time."

Joel Boulder scowled at his patient. "I didn't say any such thing, Will. I want you back on crutches for at least a week, and at that time we'll take another look at the knee and go from there. I'm not making any promises." Looking very grim, he added, "You had better listen to Vanessa. If you don't, you're not going to live to retire."

Iron started to argue but was cut short when the infirmary door opened and Jim Stenzel entered the room, carrying a sheaf of newspapers over his arm. "What've you got there, Jim?"

"A box of these was delivered to the office. A note on the outside of the carton said they're for you and the people of Casper from Bernie Tripp. Complimentary copies of the *Police Gazette*."

As he spoke Stenzel flashed a copy at his boss. The front page was graced with an artist's sketch of Will Iron underneath a headline declaring, SHERIFF WILL IRON HUNTS KILLER DOWN LIKE MAD DOG . . . KILLER TAKES COWARD'S WAY OUT.

"The story of your hunting down Vic Maynard and his leap into the canyon is right here on page one,

Will," Jim said proudly, "and your biography takes up the entire second page."

The sheriff sighed uncomfortably and shook his head, mumbling, "I wish Tripp hadn't made such a big story out of it."

A loud knock sounded at the door. Council chairman Ty Miller stuck his head in the room, asking if he could enter. When the doctor gave permission, Miller came in, expressing his concern for the lawman. "Will, people who saw the gunfight told me you almost got yourself killed. I've contacted the county officials and told them about it. We want you to meet with us tonight at the town hall, at eight o'clock. We request that Vanessa and Jim be there, too."

Iron knew they would be asking for his resignation but reluctantly agreed to be there.

That evening, as soon as everyone had arrived at the town hall and was seated, Ty Miller explained the reason for the meeting. "I think we're all agreed that after a long and illustrious career, it's time for Will Iron to step down as sheriff of Natrona County. I've been in conversation with Dr. Joel Boulder to get the facts about Sheriff Iron's injury, and the doctor's feelings are that the sheriff should retire from law enforcement before the knee causes his death."

Miller waited for the rumble of voices to die down, then looked at Iron, who was frowning. "Will, I'm sure you know that everyone in this room respects you and deeply appreciates the fine job you've done all these years. Only the Lord in heaven knows how many times you've laid your life on the line to save ours." He paused briefly, then went on, "I don't like this any better than you do, but in the light of what happened to your knee in that shoot-out today, we're all respectfully asking you to hand in your badge. We're concerned that next time you won't be so lucky, and either you'll be killed or some of our citizens will be."

Tears trickled down Vanessa's cheeks. Iron looked into her eyes, which silently pleaded with him, then said hesitantly, "Gentlemen . . . this is the hardest thing I've ever had to do . . . but it appears that for the good of everyone concerned, I should bow to your wishes. . . . Very well. I will turn in my badge as soon as Jim is elected sheriff."

Miller smiled, looked at Stenzel, and said, "Your boss wants you to inherit his badge, Jim. Are you willing? It will take about ten days to set up an election. It'll only be a formality since no one will be running against you, but it must be done that way."

"I accept," Stenzel replied, grinning broadly.

"Good." Miller smiled at Iron. "Now, I have the pleasure of informing you that in consideration of all the years you've looked after us, Will, the county board wishes to grant you a year's salary to give you time to find another way to make a living."

Vanessa squeezed her husband's hand. Brushing away her tears, she murmured, "Darling, I know how hard this is for you, but I hope you'll try and see this not as the end of something but as a wonderful new beginning."

Iron drew her closer and sighed. "I'll try, Vanessa. I'll try."

The news was quickly printed in the *Casper Herald*, and word of the upcoming election spread. On the day before the election, Sheriff Will Iron and his deputy were glancing out the open door of their office when a handsome, blond-haired man of about thirty hauled up out front and dismounted, then approached. Tall, broad-shouldered, and muscular, the stranger paused in the doorway and asked with a smile, "Will Iron and Jim Stenzel, right?"

"Correct," Iron confirmed with a nod, rising from his chair behind the desk. "And you are . . . ?"

Jim Stenzel stood also as the stranger stepped in, extended his hand, and replied, "Jack Lancaster."

They all shook hands, and Iron gestured at the chair on the opposite side of his desk. When Lancaster was seated, Iron leaned across the desk and asked, "Now, what can we do for you?"

Stroking his mustache, Lancaster replied, "I'm from down Denver way, Sheriff. I read about your retirement and Deputy Stenzel's upcoming election in the *Rocky Mountain News*. I also read that article about you in the *Police Gazette*. Since Mr. Stenzel is to become sheriff tomorrow, I'd like to apply for the job as his deputy."

Iron flicked a glance at Stenzel, then studied Lancaster for a long moment. The man was well built and looked tough. He could probably give a good account of himself in a fight. Finally the seasoned lawman said, "Well, it's up to Jim who he hires. How much law enforcement experience do you have?"

Lancaster reddened. Clearing his throat, he answered, "Well, Sheriff, to be honest, I haven't had any experience behind a badge. But hear me out, okay?"

Iron nodded silently, giving his deputy a furtive smile.

Lancaster explained that his greatest desire had always been to wear a badge but that he had been tied down until quite recently, having to run his aging father's ranch. Upon his father's death a few weeks before, Lancaster had sold the ranch, deciding that his chance had finally come to get into law enforcement. When he read the article about Iron's retirement in the Denver newspaper, he had hopped on his horse and headed for Casper, hoping to get the job as Stenzel's deputy.

Looking squarely at the older lawman, Lancaster said,

"I know taking on a fella with no experience may seem like a risk, but I'd take the deputy's job with no salary until Mr. Stenzel felt I was worthy of it. I've got money from the sale of the ranch to live on."

Stenzel remarked, "Being tough with outlaws and miscreants is a whole lot different from being tough with stubborn cattle—or even ranch hands, for that matter. How good are you with that gun on your hip?"

"I'll show you if you'll give me the chance," the newcomer promised.

Stenzel agreed to let Lancaster show him what he could do with the sidearm. Taking the two lawmen outside of town, Jack Lancaster amazed them with his speed and accuracy.

Impressed, Iron said, "Jim, I'd advise you to hire this fella if you can get a good character reference from someone of import in Denver."

As they mounted up and settled in their saddles, Lancaster asked, "How would a reference from a fellow lawman suit you?"

Stenzel raised his eyebrows. "A lawman?"

"Yeah. Denver's sheriff, Bob Kasten, was a very close friend of my father's."

"Couldn't beat that," Stenzel mused. "Let's get back to town. I'll wire him right away."

Late that afternoon, a return telegram arrived for Jim Stenzel from Denver County Sheriff Bob Kasten, stating that Jack Lancaster was a man of unquestionably sound and good character. His recommendation was that Lancaster be hired for the job.

At the close of election day, a swearing-in ceremony was held in front of the sheriff's office for Jim Stenzel. Will Iron removed his badge and proudly pinned it on the young man he had hired and trained. Standing beside her husband, Vanessa Iron cried with joy now that her husband would no longer face danger. Several merchants immediately offered Iron positions in their shops, and a couple of local ranchers approached him with offers of jobs on their spreads. But the ex-sheriff explained that he was going to let his knee heal for a few months before he took up a new career.

The day after the election, Sheriff Jim Stenzel hired Jack Lancaster and began training him for his old job.

Two days after that, a pair of rough-looking men rode stealthily into Casper, heading to the alley that ran parallel to Main Street. After tying up their horses, Mickey Swafford and Junior Owens made their way down a passageway between the two buildings that stood opposite the sheriff's office. There they hid in the shadows, maintaining a vigil on the office across the street. It was ten o'clock in the morning.

Whispering to his friend, Owens said, "Sooner or later that deputy's gonna come out of the office or come down the street and go into it. Whichever it is—and whenever it is—he's gonna die! Nobody shoots down my brother and gets away with it!"

The twosome waited patiently, ready to cut down Jim Stenzel. Twice a husky blond man wearing a badge came and went, but there was no sign of the man who had killed Hank Owens.

Nearly an hour and a half had passed when suddenly Junior Owens elbowed Swafford and said urgently, "There he is!"

The new sheriff strode slowly up the street, greeting passersby. Stenzel finally reached his office door and was about to enter when Harley Carter, the bank president, caught up to the young lawman to offer his congratulations. Stenzel turned from the door to smile at the well-wisher when Swafford and Owens opened fire, their hail of bullets shattering the office window and cutting the two men down. Women screamed and men shouted as Carter, shot through the head, crumpled immediately while Stenzel gamely reached for his revolver before taking a couple of slugs. He fell to the boardwalk in a heap, blood pumping from his wounds.

Satisfied that their deadly mission had been accomplished, Owens and Swafford ran for their horses. As the twosome emerged from between the buildings and leapt onto their saddles, three men who were hurrying along the alley, drawn by the shouts and cries from Main Street, stared at the fleeing assassins.

Owens swore and lashed his horse, shouting, "Come on, Mickey! Let's get outta here!" With that, both men galloped away.

When they were well beyond the northern edge of town, Owens signaled to stop. They drew rein in a cloud of dust, and Junior said, "Those three men can identify us, Mickey! We've gotta head for high country!"

Swafford agreed. Spurring their mounts savagely, they headed directly for the mountains.

Will Iron had been at home, working in the yard, at the time the gunfire had erupted. Freezing at his chore, he was looking toward Main Street when Vanessa appeared at the front door. The ex-sheriff threw down the rake in his hand and said anxiously, "Honey, I've got to go see what's happened."

"No, you don't!" she countered, coming out the door. "You're not wearing a badge anymore, remember?"

"I know, but Jim may be involved. I've got to see if he needs me."

Not waiting for her to respond, Iron started toward the street. His wife caught up to him, saying, "You're not going without me!"

The Irons reached Main Street and learned, to their horror, that Harley Carter had been killed and Jim Stenzel shot. Joel Boulder was kneeling beside the new sheriff, examining the wounds, as Iron pushed his way through the crowd with Vanessa. He looked down at Carter, shaking his head sadly, then knelt beside Stenzel. "How bad is he, Doc?" he asked the physician.

Boulder looked up and replied, "One bullet seared his side and broke two ribs, another one grazed his head, and a third one caught him in the shoulder. He was lucky. Whoever tried to kill him was a lousy shot. Missed anything vital. As it is, he'll be laid up for several weeks. Only problem is, we won't have an experienced lawman around."

Iron did not comment on the last remark. Turning to Deputy Jack Lancaster, who stood nearby, he asked, "Anybody see who did it?"

"Yes, sir," Lancaster replied. "I have three men here who saw an unsavory-looking pair running from between the buildings where the shots were fired." He paused and turned, then gestured at a middle-aged rancher and his wife. "And this couple saw the same pair riding hell-for-leather north toward the mountains."

Wrath toward the gunmen who had killed the banker and shot down his friend welled up in Will Iron. His face burning with passion, he growled, "I'm going after them. I can't let them get away with this!"

Vanessa gasped, "No, Will! You're not a lawman anymore!"

Looking around, Iron spotted Ty Miller standing in the crowd. "Ty, you can deputize me. I've got to bring those murderers in!"

The physician stared at the ex-lawman. "Will, are you forgetting that bad knee? You can't do it."

"Will, please!" Vanessa cried. "Listen to him!"

"Vanessa, I have to do this. And if Ty won't deputize me, I'll go on my own!" Iron snapped. "Those killers must be punished!"

"All right, I'll deputize you if you insist," Miller said, relenting, "but take a posse."

Iron shook his head. "They're heading into the mountains. I can do a better job of tracking without a dozen men tagging along. Let's get me deputized so I'll have the authority to arrest those two."

Vanessa gripped her husband's arm and begged, "Will, why not let Deputy Lancaster form a posse and go after them?"

"No good, honey," Iron argued. "Jack's just too inexperienced to take on a task like this. We can ask Marshal Tom Harrison over in Powder River to come here as acting sheriff. He's got a deputy who can take over for him."

While Vanessa looked on, her face pale and drawn, Iron was quickly sworn in. Just before Jim Stenzel was carried over to the clinic, he removed his badge and handed it over to its original owner, who smiled and promised, "I'll give this back to you real soon, Jim."

Sending Jack Lancaster for his stabled horse, Iron then hurried home with Vanessa to pack his saddlebags. She tried fruitlessly to persuade him to change his mind, finally giving up.

When Lancaster arrived leading Iron's horse, he was riding his own. "The way I see it," he reasoned, "since I'm too inexperienced to act as sheriff and the marshal from Powder River would be here for that assignment, I'd like to go along with you. That way, if something were to happen to that knee of yours, I would be there to help."

"Oh, Will, please say yes!" Vanessa begged.

Iron nodded. "All right. Fact is, I might need some help." He smiled at Lancaster, adding, "Besides, this pursuit will give you a chance to learn to track down fugitives."

The deputy smiled. "I hear you're plenty good at tracking men, Sheriff."

Stepping outside, Iron took his filled saddlebags from

Vanessa and buckled them to his saddle. His Colt .45 was on his hip, and his rifle was in the saddle boot. While the deputy looked on, Iron kissed a tearful and worried Vanessa good-bye, saying, "Now, darlin', don't you fret. I'm going to be all right." He kissed her again, told her he loved her, and swung into the saddle.

The two lawmen trotted up the street side by side. When they reached the corner, Iron looked back over his shoulder. Vanessa still stood there, watching him. He gave her a brief wave, then heeled his horse and rode off.

Chapter Ten

Riding hard, Junior Owens and Mickey Swafford had passed the foothills of the Rockies and had started to climb by the time the sun began to set behind the towering peaks ahead. Their plan was to cross the mountains and head for the Teton Forest in western Wyoming, where they would hole up until the heat was off.

Coming around a tree-studded hump after a long ascent, they were suddenly upon a campsite where eight rough-looking men were gathered. One of the men was busy building a campfire, but the others were immediately on their feet and holding cocked guns on the two riders.

Owens pulled rein and Swafford followed suit. Splaying his hands, Owens said quickly, "Hold it, fellas! We just happened along. We don't mean no harm."

"They don't look like lawmen, Luke," the man at the fire observed. "Leastwise I ain't never seen no lawmen that looked that scabby. They look more like our kind."

"What's your kind?" Owens asked.

The leader stepped closer and looked the pair over carefully. "You two on the dodge?"

Owens and Swafford looked at each other, silently agreeing that they were among friends. Owens nodded and admitted, "Yeah."

"Good," the leader said, grinning. "Climb down and

have supper with us. My name's Luke Coffey. Man here at the fire is Jess Hall." Gesturing at each of the other men, he ticked off their names: "Norm Whitney, Albert Norberg, Willie Fryar, Harvey Smith, Ted Lynch . . . and the big, ugly monster is Yale Chitwood."

The description was no exaggeration. Chitwood stood over six and a half feet and weighed some three hundred pounds. As the newcomers dismounted, Coffey remarked, "We ain't heard your handles."

"I'm Junior Owens and my pal is Mickey Swafford."

"Howdy. Well, have a seat. Jess'll have our grub ready in no time."

Owens nodded, and he and his cohort sat down on a fallen log. Looking at Coffey, whose face glowed orange from the flickering fire, Owens asked, "You boys runnin' from the law, too?"

"Yep," Coffey replied, pulling out cigarette makings. "We gave the slip to a couple of federal marshals up in Montana a week ago. Headin' south for New Mexico."

"What'd you do?"

Coffey shrugged. "We robbed a couple of banks and killed a U.S. marshal up by Helena."

Swafford elbowed Owens. "We really are your kind," he said to the others. "We took down the deputy in Casper this mornin'," he bragged.

"Casper!" Coffey gasped. "That's Will Iron's town."

"So you know about Iron, do you?" Owens put in.

Coffey snorted. "Who don't?" His face turned to stone, and his voice was a growl as he continued, "Will Iron killed a close friend of mine a couple of years ago in Casper. I hate his guts for it." He paused a moment, then noted, "But I sure wouldn't want to tangle with him. Where'd you boys get the nerve to take out his deputy? I take it Iron was out of town at the time."

Owens chuckled. "We didn't stick around long enough to find out."

After the meal, the newcomers told the others they would pull out after breakfast. They then unrolled their bedrolls and slept well, feeling safe with the outlaw gang.

The two fugitives were still asleep as dawn began to brighten the Wyoming sky. Willie Fryar awakened before the others and climbed farther up, into the trees, to relieve himself. His vantage point gave him a clear view to the east, and his attention was drawn to two riders who were making the climb—heading straight for the camp. By squinting, he was able to make out badges on the riders' chests. Then he recognized Will Iron.

Swearing under his breath, he ran down to the grassy spot and began shaking Owens and Swafford, saying, "You guys gotta get outta here fast! Iron and a deputy are ridin' this way!"

The whole camp came to life as the outlaws scrambled from their bedrolls. While the two fugitives leapt into their saddles, Luke Coffey said, "We'll tell Iron we never saw you fellas. Git goin'!"

"What about you?" Owens asked. "Didn't you say you took down a lawman in Helena?"

"Yeah, but we wore masks. Nobody knows who did it."

"Okay. Thanks!" Owens said fervently, and he and his cohort galloped west, disappearing quickly into the timber.

Will Iron and Jack Lancaster had ridden their mounts hard until dark, Iron's trained eye keeping them steadily on the killers' trail. While they rode, the seasoned tracker gave the novice deputy pointers on reading sign, and Lancaster was astonished by Iron's skill.

They were up just before dawn, climbing into the mountains. Iron told Lancaster that judging from the tracks the killers had left, they were closing in on the pair. Lancaster was amazed at what the ex-sheriff had taught him about tracking in such a short time.

As they started up a steep climb toward dense timber, Iron said, "I'll tell you, Jack, I sure hate to think of taking this badge off again, but you're proving to me that you've got the mettle to be a fine lawman. And the way you're picking up tracking is mighty impressive. Who knows? If Jim Stenzel ever decides to move on, you could one day be sheriff of Natrona County."

Lancaster smiled. "Thanks for the vote of confidence, Sheriff. And I really appreciate you having educated me on reading sign. It's a skill that'll come in mighty handy, I'm sure."

As they neared the top of the incline, Iron ran his gaze over the heavy stand of pines and drew rein. As Lancaster stopped beside him, the aging lawman pulled his gun and said in a low voice, "Their tracks are mingled with others here, Jack. These others aren't as fresh." He paused, then pointed. "Look!"

Smoke from a campfire began to rise above the trees. Whoever was around the bend was not making any attempt at concealment. Nudging his horse forward at a slow walk, Iron held his gun ready—as did Jack Lancaster beside him—and moved into the grassy clearing. Luke Coffey and his men were standing around the rekindled fire, acting relaxed. Noting that their weapons were in leather, Iron holstered his own gun and said, "Morning, fellas."

"Morning," chorused the unkempt bunch.

"I'm Sheriff Will Iron," the lawman announced. "This is my deputy, Jack Lancaster. Where're you fellas headed?"

Coffey gestured with his thumb over his shoulder. "New Mexico. We got hired on by a big spread down near Las Cruces as cattle punchers."

Iron nodded. "My deputy and I are chasing a pair of killers. They're dressed in range clothes like yours and moving fast. You see anybody like that?"

"Nope," Coffey replied, shaking his head. "We ain't seen nobody at all for a good couple of days."

Iron knew the man was lying. The two fugitives had been here, all right, for their tracks led straight to the spot. While Coffey was talking, the lawman studied the ground around the campfire, easing his horse a little farther so he could get a better look. After a few moments he twisted in the saddle and fixed the leader with steady eyes. "You're lying to me, mister."

Coffey's mouth dropped, and his face took on a wounded, insulted look. "I ain't lyin', Sheriff. And I don't rightly appreciate such accusations, neither."

Iron glanced around. "I count eight men here. You have some more out running around?"

"No. There's just us."

His jaw clenched, Iron railed, "Look, I don't want to hear any more cock-and-bull stories. The grass is matted down in ten places where men slept. I know the killers slept in your camp last night. Their tracks led right here. Now, what kind of story did they tell you?"

Every man in the gang stood mute, eyes riveted on their leader.

Coffey's face was a mixture of hatred and fear, and his fists repeatedly opened and closed. But he said and did nothing, merely staring at Will Iron.

Iron glared at Coffey with disgust, warning him, "There's a stiff penalty in this state for abetting outlaws. You're lucky I don't have time to run you in and look up any wanteds on you—and you better hope I don't ever ride across your path again." Wheeling his horse around, he rode to the far end of the camp and examined the ground. Then he called to the deputy, "Come on, Jack. They went this way."

Lancaster spurred his mount to catch up, taking a long, last look back at the men in the camp before passing from view.

Junior Owens and Mickey Swafford pushed their horses hard as they climbed through dense forest, knowing Will Iron was hot on their trail. When they stopped to let the lathered, blowing horses have a brief rest, Owens said, "Mickey, we're gonna have to outsmart those two lawmen and kill 'em. I've got an idea."

"I hope it's a good one, Junior," Swafford muttered. "Them two are bound to be mighty close."

"It *is* a good one," Owens asserted. "The first overhanging limb we come to that I can reach, I'll grab it and swing out of the saddle. Then I'll climb down the tree and hide in the brush. There'll be no way Iron could know that I ain't on my horse no more, right? He and his deputy'll continue to follow both horses. Then as soon as they pass me, I'll shoot 'em in the back. Simple, huh?"

Swafford grinned. "I got to hand it to you, Junior: That's real good thinkin'."

The killers mounted up and spurred their horses through the woods. A few moments later the perfect limb presented itself, and Owens grabbed it and hauled himself up, letting his horse keep moving. Dangling, he instructed, "Just keep ridin', Mick. When you hear the shots, turn around and come on back."

Going hand over hand on the limb, Owens reached the tree trunk and shinnied down quickly. Pulling his revolver but not cocking it, he took off at a run, looking around for a place to hide, but his feet tangled in an exposed root, and he fell hard to the grassy ground as his weapon flew out of his hand. Cursing his clumsiness, he scrambled to his feet and looked around for his gun. He found it lying in a large puddle. He swore angrily. There was a good chance now that the weapon would not fire. Having no time to find out for sure, he continued on.

Some ten minutes later the sheriff and his deputy came along at a steady trot. Just after they passed the tree where Owens had swung from the saddle, the sharp-eyed lawman spied the matted-down grass just ahead and figured out what was going on. Drawing rein, he told Lancaster what he had deduced, instructing, "Jack, since it's hard for me to move on foot, you dismount and go after our ambusher; I'll go after his partner. Be careful. You know how to follow his footprints, don't you?"

Excitement was showing on the deputy's face. "Sure do, thanks to you, Sheriff. Don't worry. I'm gonna get him."

"I like your attitude," Iron said, grinning. "See you when I bring the other one back."

The object of the sheriff's pursuit, Mickey Swafford, was leading his friend's horse through the trees, climbing higher. Reaching a rocky plateau, he stopped and looked back just in time to see the two lawmen split up, with the deputy disappearing into the woods while Iron continued on.

Swafford swore. Where was Owens? Maybe something had happened to him—or maybe his gun jammed. *I guess it's up to me to get Iron,* he told himself. *I'll hide the horses and set up my own ambush.*

More than a half hour after Will Iron and Jack Lancaster had split up, the sheriff spotted the place where Mickey Swafford had pulled the horses into the dense woods. His seasoned senses suddenly warned him he was about to be ambushed, and he dived from the saddle—a split second before a shot rang out.

Pain ripped through his left knee as he hit the ground

hard, and he winced, fighting back the need to scream. Rolling behind a tree, he drew his gun. A second shot came, chewing into the bark just above his head.

Iron peered around the other side of the tree in time to see Swafford dart through the brush, trying to get into a better position to fire at him. The lawman popped a shot at him, just missing, but Swafford stumbled and fell. Forgetting his knee in the excitement of the moment, Iron sprang after the killer, and his leg crumpled under him, sending him sprawling. He dragged himself behind a huge, fallen log and listened carefully. He could hear the outlaw coming toward him through the brush, breathing hard.

Iron lay pressed up against the log, holding his gun cocked. The hard breathing and heavy footfalls came closer. The lawman tensed, ready to take his man alive or dead. Suddenly Swafford was looming above him, on the opposite side of the log, and looking around.

The outlaw jerked with a start when Iron said in a quiet, even voice, "Don't move, mister, or you're dead." Swafford's hands flinched slightly, and the experienced lawman could tell that the man was weighing his chances of killing Iron. "Don't do it," the sheriff cautioned. "Throw your gun out in front of you."

The young outlaw made the wrong decision. When he started to swing his weapon, Iron's gun roared. The bullet struck Owens under his bearded chin and exited through the top of his head. He collapsed behind the log in a lifeless heap.

With effort Iron struggled to his feet and stood looking down at the dead killer. "Your kind never learn, do they?" he muttered, shaking his head.

Iron was startled as a gun suddenly boomed directly behind him. Bringing his Colt .45 around, ready to fire, he was stunned to see Junior Owens stiffen and fall, a cocked revolver in his hand. Jack Lancaster stepped out of the shadows, holding a smoking gun. It was obvious that the killer had been about to shoot Iron in the back.

Favoring his leg, Iron headed toward his deputy. He sighed with relief and smiled, saying, "Whew! That was close. Thanks, Jack. You just saved my hide!"

Lancaster's face abruptly turned hard. His eyes were cold and deadly as he aimed the still-smoking gun at the sheriff. "Drop your Colt and get your hands in the air," he ordered.

A cold ball formed in Iron's stomach and a tingle went over his scalp. Stunned, he stood as though mesmerized, unable to believe his eyes and ears. Fixing the blond deputy with a penetrating stare, he finally demanded, "What is this?"

Lancaster's face was grim. "This is revenge, that's what. Now, drop your gun."

Iron's color darkened. Letting his Colt fall and raising his hands shoulder high, he commanded, "Out with it! What's this all about, Lancaster?"

The deputy's mouth curled into a sneer. Laughing mirthlessly, he said, "My name isn't Lancaster. It's Maynard. You're familiar with that name, aren't you? I'm Vance. Maybe you heard my father speak of me. You knew my father, of course . . . Vic Maynard."

"Then you're Vic's oldest son."

"That's right."

"But how—?"

"How'd I manage to pass myself off as Jack Lancaster? Actually, it was real easy. Luck was on my side. See, I happened to pick up a copy of the *Police Gazette* while in town one day—'town' being Kearney, Nebraska. I read the headlines, and I read the story." His voice hardened. "The *real* story. The whole truth and nothing but . . . not that fairy tale that you wrote me. I came here to get even with you for what you did to my father. As fate would have it, I met the real Jack Lancaster when I stopped for a drink in a Nebraska town called McCook. The man having a drink beside me at the bar was a rancher like me. He gave me a brief account of himself—just as I gave it to you, including his dead father's friendship with the sheriff in Denver." He chuckled coldly. "The difference was Lancaster was heading east to start a new life."

Maynard glared at the lawman. "So I decided to use his identity . . . and it worked perfectly. Now I get even with you for hunting down my father like an animal and forcing him to leap over that cliff."

"You've got it all wrong. It wasn't like that," Iron protested. "If you read the reporter's story in the *Gazette* then you know that."

"Shut up!" Maynard roared. "I know exactly how it was! My father wouldn't have killed himself if you hadn't driven him to it. He had no reason to kill himself. That cock-and-bull story about him murdering two black-mailers . . . I knew my father. He wouldn't have kept anything from us. If he had once served time, he would have told us. He knew how much we loved him." His eyes narrowed dangerously. "You as much as killed him. He was innocent. Now I'm gonna do to you what you did to my dad."

Iron's gaze was steady as he asked, "If you wanted to get even, why didn't you let this outlaw shoot me in the back? Or why didn't *you* do it and have it done?"

Scowling, Maynard spat, "Oh, no! You don't get off so easy. You hounded my father to death; I'm gonna hound you to death."

Iron's mind was racing, trying to figure a way to overpower Maynard. He had no idea what the man had in mind, but he would have to act fast.

Before he could do anything, however, Maynard called out, "Okay, fellas! You can come out now!"

Iron felt his blood turn cold when the eight outlaws

from the camp suddenly emerged from a nearby thicket. He could not keep the shock from showing on his face.

Maynard laughed and said, "Talk about fate, Sheriff. While I was supposed to be chasing down the fella that was on foot, I doubled back to the camp and offered Mr. Coffey and his pals some money to help me. It was pretty obvious to me—as I'm sure it was to you—that they aren't cowhands. They're owlhoots. I also found out that Mr. Coffey hates your guts because you killed a friend of his in a gunfight. Since Luke has this hatred burning in him, and since all these boys like money, they've agreed to help me play a game. A game of hunting . . . and you're the prey."

A cold dread came over Will Iron. He had known fear many a time in his long career behind a badge, but this situation was the worst. Maynard was going to turn him loose, then run him down. With his bad knee, he would be terribly handicapped. What kind of chance would he have of surviving with nine men after him?

Maynard broke into his thoughts. "This turned out even better than I had planned. I figured on playing the game alone, and even though I knew I'd be going up against your years of experience, my need for revenge was enough for me to gamble on winning. But, like I said, fate stepped in yet again. I figure it'll be a lot safer for me—and even more fun—with these men to help me."

Iron thought of how Vanessa had begged him to let "Jack Lancaster" take a posse and go after the two killers. He wondered how fate would have handled Maynard's game if he had listened to Vanessa. He also wondered what Maynard would do if he realized that these were the very mountains where his father had died.

Maynard bent and picked up Iron's Colt .45. Jamming it under his belt, he said, "I'll tell you what. I'm gonna give you a real sporting chance. You've got two hours to run before we come after you. The *Police Gazette* said you're real good as the hunter; let's see how good you are as the *hunted*."

The lawman knew it would do no good to try to talk Vance Maynard out of his insane plan. He would have to somehow win, even though the odds were stacked overwhelmingly against him.

Maynard pulled out a pocket watch. Checking it, he announced, "It's seven-twenty. At nine-twenty the hunters will start after their prey." Shoving the timepiece back in his pocket, he grinned demonically and hissed, "You've already wasted five seconds, Sheriff. I'd suggest you start running."

Iron's gray eyes smoldered as he stared unwaveringly at Maynard for a long moment. Then, without a word, he turned and limped westward, heading into higher country.

Vance Maynard and the Coffey gang watched the hated lawman until he was out of sight. When the sound of his progress through the pines was no longer audible, Maynard said to the gang leader, "Luke, send one of your men back down the mountain with all the horses, including Iron's and mine. We'll do the tracking on foot."

Coffey looked at him incredulously. "On foot? Why?"

"Because we're dealing with a man who knows his way around these mountains probably better than anyone. I want those horses gone so he won't be able to double back and steal one for an easy escape. Besides, if we go on foot, it'll be more sporting—and I want the satisfaction of knowing he had a sporting chance before I cornered him and killed him."

Nodding stiffly, Coffey called over one of his men, telling him to take all the horses straight east down the mountain. Albert Norberg was to wait there until they met up with him later.

With his knee throbbing and sweat beading his face, Will Iron headed up the trail . . . the very same one Vic Maynard had taken weeks ago. Iron's plan was to make his way to the Calvert cabin. A friend of the Calverts had notified the lawman that he would be going to the cabin to take the possessions—including the bay mare—at the end of the month.

The lawman assumed the mare would still be there. Given that she had enough forage, a source of water, and shelter, chances were good that she had not attempted leaping the fence and had been content to stay put in familiar surroundings. There was always the outside possibility of wolves, but the pasture was big enough that she could maintain a safe distance, should a pack have ventured near. Since wolves ordinarily kept well away from human habitation, however, and the Calverts had lived in their cabin for many years, Iron felt certain that a pack would give the place a wide berth. The lawman prayed hard that he was right. He needed the mare to get away from the madman pursuing him.

His heart pounded as he climbed higher, and the pain in his reinjured knee was almost unbearable. After traveling about a half mile, he veered off the trail, cursing himself for teaching the impostor so much about reading sign. He would have to do his best to leave none.

During the two-hour wait, Vance Maynard went over the deal with the gang, who sat around, anxious to get started. He moved among them, eyeing each man. "As I told you before, for agreeing to help I'll give you each two hundred dollars. I didn't figure on needing that kind of money, so I don't have it with me, of course.

But as soon as this little job is over, we'll go back to town and I'll get it for you. Is that acceptable?"

The outlaws all agreed.

"Good. Now, the eight of us will go in pairs after Iron. Whichever team finds him and corners him will get a bonus—a thousand dollars per man." He grinned at the gang's eager response. "And don't worry. I've got plenty of money in the Casper bank. When I return to town, I'll sadly announce that the killers we were chasing caught us off guard, that they tied me up and took off with Iron, and I have no idea where they went or what they've done with him. I'll act frightened and turn in my badge, saying this lawman's life is not for me after all. I'll withdraw my money and then I'll just mount up and head for home—meeting you fellas at a prearranged spot, of course."

Pacing back and forth in front of the motley bunch, Maynard told them, "Now, I want to emphasize that you're not to kill Iron, just corner or capture him. The killing of the man will be my pleasure—after I've administered a little torture. I owe him for what he did to my father, and it's gonna be me who pays the debt." Fixing each man with a hard look, he warned, "If one of you kills Iron, the bonus to you *and* your partner will be forfeited. The main object of the game is to make Will Iron run for his life, just as he made Vic Maynard do." His mien softened, and he asked, "Any questions?"

Yale Chitwood rose to his feet. Towering over the blond man, he grunted, "Yeah, I got one. How do we know you really have the money in the bank and you ain't gonna cheat us?"

Grinning up at him, Vance replied, "You'll just have to take my word for it."

Luke Coffey took a drag on his cigarette, then said, "It'll be okay, Yale. Vance is our kind. We can trust him." He stood and walked over to Maynard and slung an arm around his shoulder. "Matter of fact, I trust him so much, I'm gonna team with him. That okay with you, Vance?"

"Suits me just fine."

"Good," Coffey responded. "Okay, here's how I see the other teams: Hall and Chitwood will be one, Lynch and Whitney another, and Fryar and Smith the third."

Maynard smiled his approval, then said, "When Iron is caught, those who catch him will signal the others by firing one shot, then two. Do it over and over at regular intervals so the others can locate you. As you know, sound echoes in these mountains, so it's very difficult to tell where it's coming from."

Maynard had the outlaws drag the bodies of Mickey Swafford and Junior Owens over to a deep ravine, shoving them in so they would never be found. Finally, when the two hours had expired, the hunters fanned out and set off in pursuit.

Chapter Eleven

Will Iron climbed hard and fast in the direction of the Calvert cabin. While stopping on a high perch to catch his breath and rest his injured knee, he looked behind him and saw two of Coffey's men coming up the mountainside on foot. They had not seen him yet, but he was in an open place where he would be easy to spot. Hurrying to get out of sight, he stepped awkwardly, and his knee buckled.

He was struggling to get up when he was spotted by the twosome. He heard Ted Lynch shout, "Norm! There he is!"

In Lynch's excitement, he forgot Vance Maynard's rule. Drawing his gun, he aimed at Iron and fired.

Iron was scurrying for cover and dragging his bad leg when Lynch's bullet hummed past his head. Distracted, he looked up and tripped over a boulder, then fell out of sight. He heard Lynch shout, "I got him!"

Hunkering behind the boulder, Iron heard the two men scrambling up the trail, Whitney railing at his partner for his stupidity and reminding him of Maynard's command not to kill Iron, but instead to capture him so Maynard could do the killing. "If you've killed him, Ted," Norm Whitney snarled, "I'm gonna break you in two! My bonus money'd be lost on account of your thick head!"

Iron knew his only hope was to trap his immediate pursuers. On the ground nearby was a squirrel, balancing a pinecone in its paws, intent on finding the nuts. An idea struck the lawman. Looking around, he picked up a rock, then hurled it hard at the little animal. His throw was accurate. The squirrel lay on the ground, stunned. Reaching for it, he killed it quickly, then took a sharp rock and sliced into the carcass, making a trail with its blood into deep shade a few yards away. The resourceful sheriff then picked up a stout broken tree limb, hefting it like a club, and waited behind a tree.

Breathing hard, Lynch and Whitney arrived at the spot where Iron had fallen. "Look!" Lynch gasped. "Blood! I hit him, all right! And his trail goes into the trees. Come on!"

Guns drawn, the outlaws followed the bloody trail without caution, obviously thinking Iron was badly wounded and knowing he was unarmed.

Lynch was two steps ahead of his partner as they plunged into the gloom of the dense pines. Suddenly, Iron swung his crude weapon, catching the man square on the forehead. He went down like a poleaxed steer. Before Whitney could act, the club caught him savagely across the bridge of the nose.

Limping over to the unconscious men, Iron sat them up against two adjacent trees with their hands behind them and tied them to the trunks using their belts and shirts. Taking their revolvers, he headed up the mountain.

Scattered across the face of the mountain, the three remaining teams continued their search for Will Iron. Hearing the shot, Vance Maynard and Luke Coffey halted, breathlessly waiting for more shots. All was quiet except for a soft wind and birds chattering in the trees. The two men eyed each other, puzzlement on their faces, then looked around anxiously, hoping to see something that would catch their attention. But they could not determine where the sound had come from.

Breaking the silence, Coffey said, "I'm not sure, but I think it was off to the left, only higher up."

"Yeah, I sorta thought so, too . . . but I wouldn't swear to it," Maynard responded. "Like I said before, these mountains can fool you." After a brief pause, he mused, "Why do you suppose there was just one shot? I mean, if one of your boys did lose his good sense for a minute and shot Iron, they'd have signaled by now."

Coffey pointed out, "Yeah, but there could be other people up here in these mountains. The shot might have nothin' to do with Iron."

Maynard's look of concern faded. "You're right. I hadn't thought of that."

"Don't you worry, pal," Coffey said, "we'll catch him."

As the twosome moved laterally along a rocky ridge, a frustrated Maynard remarked, "Why haven't we seen some sign of him?"

Coffey chuckled and replied, "Didn't you tell me the man is an expert at readin' sign?"

"Yes."

"Well, then it stands to reason that he'd be pretty good at *not leavin'* sign."

Maynard swore. "He's a man, ain't he? He's got to leave some kind of trace."

Veering off to the left, Maynard and Coffey continued to climb. Close to half an hour had passed when a bloodcurdling scream from not too far above them brought them to an abrupt halt.

Eyes wide, Vance Maynard turned to his partner and said with a tremor, "That was a human scream. A man's."

Coffey was nodding when the air was filled with another scream—the tone pitched differently from the first, indicating a second man—followed by a wild roar.

Coffey pulled his gun, saying, "That's a bear, Vance!

Probably a grizzly! I've seen 'em and heard 'em before, in the mountains of Montana!"

A chill slithered down Vance Maynard's spine as screams of stark terror echoed across the mountain. His face was white as he looked at Coffey and gasped, "That bear's got two men, Luke! We've got to find them!"

Another vicious roar blended with more screams. The outlaw leader looked at the revolver in his hand and said weakly, "We can't take on a grizzly with these peashooters, Vance! We—"

More screams cut off Coffey's words. There was one final wild roar, and then all was quiet.

"Okay, now," Coffey half-whispered, "we gotta get up there. But be real, real quiet. Keep your gun ready. If we run into that grizzly, shoot for the head. It's the only chance we'll have."

Climbing steadily, sweat pouring down their faces and bodies, the two men cautiously made their way toward where they thought the awful sounds had come from. They followed a steep trail to the large boulder, and when they reached it, Coffey pointed at the ground and said, "Look, Vance. Blood! It leads up there into those trees. Careful, now."

Maynard and Coffey inched their way into the dark shade of the timber, following the trail of squirrel blood that Will Iron had earlier left for his pursuers. Moments later they froze in their tracks, gaping at the appalling scene before them: Lynch and Whitney, helplessly bound to two trees, had been ripped to shreds by a grizzly, which was busy feasting on their bodies. The ground beneath them was soaked with blood, and the bear's fur was smeared and sticky. The corpses, including the faces, had been mangled almost beyond recognition.

Dumbstruck and nauseated as well as fearful that the bear would become aware of their presence, Maynard and Coffey backed away into the trees. But the grizzly sensed them and turned. Standing up on his hind legs, it sniffed the air, then spotted the intruders. It let out a deafening roar, then charged.

The two men blasted away, but their terror spoiled their aim. The bear kept coming, and the ground fairly rumbled with its progress. Finally, with the huge animal just yards away, Maynard and Coffey managed to put a couple of bullets into the grizzly's brain, and it fell with a thud, almost at their feet. It snorted weakly a couple of times, then lay still.

Maynard abruptly bent over double, his face devoid of color, and began heaving. Recovering, he looked at Coffey with watery eyes.

The gang leader's complexion was a ghastly pale green, and cold sweat was beaded on his forehead. Coffey managed to choke out, "Lynch and Whitney were my friends. The grizzly killed 'em, but they were tied to the trees by human hands. *Iron's* hands." A strangled curse came from his throat, followed by a string of vile names heaped on the lawman's head. His face bloated with hatred, he wheezed furiously, "That filthy scum left them helpless! Just as heartless as the way he treated your father! The man's an animal, Vance. He's gonna rue the day he was born when I get my hands on him!"

Maynard's face was grim with determination. "Let's go. The quicker we catch that murdering dog, the better I'll like it."

As they climbed on, Maynard said, "Luke, I just thought of something. Did you see Lynch and Whitney's guns back there?"

Coffey stopped short and stared at his partner. Swearing, he spat, "No! That means he's got two guns now. He'll be able to fight back."

Jess Hall and Yale Chitwood were zigzagging their way up the mountain, searching hard for some indication that they were on Will Iron's trail, when they heard the series of shots. Chitwood turned to his partner. "Whaddya suppose them shots were? They was too many for the signal."

Hall shook his head. Looking up at his huge crony, he replied, "Maybe we should go back and find out."

Chitwood's gaze drifted down the mountainside. Suddenly he squinted, peering through the trees. He was certain he had seen something. Shifting his position so as to get a better look, he focused on the spot carefully.

"See somethin'?" Hall queried, adjusting his battered hat on his head.

"Yeah," Chitwood grunted, pointing. "Somethin' moved down there by them aspens."

The twosome stared at the spot about a hundred yards below them, and suddenly they both saw him. Will Iron was stumbling his way upward, weaving among the timber.

"Well, what do you know?" the huge man said, chuckling. "Seems we must've passed him, Jess. Let's just cut across over here and head him off. We'll fix up a little surprise for the poor, lame lawman."

As they moved laterally across the rugged mountainside, Hall laughed and said, "I can almost feel that money in my hands now, Yale!"

Chitwood snickered. "Yeah, I'm gonna find me the best saloon in Casper and get so drunk I wouldn't even know my own mother if I was to see her."

"What're you talkin' about?" Hall countered, grinning. "You ain't never had a mother!" After they had gone a bit farther, he said, "Yale, don't forget, we're not supposed to kill Iron. If you kill him, I won't get no money, either."

"Don't worry, pal," Chitwood replied. "I'll just mash him up a little. You know . . . soften him up a bit so's that Maynard guy can torture him easier."

*   *   *

Enduring the pain in his leg, Will Iron had been watching his footing on the steep path when he heard the series of shots. He stopped short and looked up. Not seeing anything, he continued on a bit farther— only to find a massive Yale Chitwood, sided by Jess Hall, blocking his path several yards away and leering down at him. They had obviously not yet noticed that Iron now had a revolver in his holster, not to mention another tucked under his belt, since neither man had his gun drawn.

It took the outlaws only a second to correct that erroneous thinking; startled, their eyes bulging, they clawed for their guns. But the lightning-fast lawman had already whipped out his revolver, and in the split second that it took him to draw, Iron had sensed that the smaller man was the faster of the two. The lawman's Colt blasted Jess Hall in the heart, and he died on his feet.

Yale Chitwood was still drawing the gun from his holster when Iron's weapon roared, and he flinched, jumping to the side. Iron pivoted slightly in order to bring the muzzle in line with Chitwood, and when he did, he twisted his leg. Pain lanced through his knee and it gave. Iron's gun discharged as he fell, the bullet tearing into a tree just behind Chitwood, chipping bark.

By this time the giant had his gun out, but he suddenly paused, then reholstered his weapon. Striding over to the lawman as Iron was bringing his gun to bear, Chitwood thrust his foot out and caught the revolver, sending it hurtling through the air.

"You killed my partner!" the giant roared.

Before Iron could pull out the weapon tucked under his belt, Chitwood's huge booted foot shot out and caught him on the jaw. The lawman fell flat, momentarily stunned.

"I've got you now, Iron," Chitwood growled. Wiping the sweat from his face, he leaned over to remove the revolver from under Iron's belt. The fallen lawman grabbed Chitwood's wrist as the outlaw's hand closed on the gun butt, struggling to keep him from getting it. The giant's sweaty hand lost its grip and the weapon slipped from his fingers. Swearing, Chitwood knocked Iron's hand away and grabbed for the gun again. The sheriff's fingers found a sharp stick lying beside him. Grabbing it, he rammed the point into Chitwood's left eye.

The huge outlaw screamed, staggering backward and clutching the stick with both hands. Iron knew the others might have heard the shot and be heading his way at that very moment. There was no time to waste. Whipping out the gun, which was still under his belt, he fired point-blank, drilling the screaming giant through the heart. Yale Chitwood fell flat on his back and died, still gripping the stick.

Iron's knee was throbbing, and his head was pulsating from the kick he had taken. He had few moments to waste, but he nonetheless took the time to empty Chitwood's gun and take the .45-caliber bullets from the man's gun belt. Stuffing them in his pocket, he retrieved the gun that had been kicked from his hand and slipped it back into his holster. Armed with both guns again, and additional ammunition, he moved on, doing his best to leave no sign.

Iron felt as though cobwebs were clinging to his brain, and the agony of his knee, which was swelling up badly, was sending waves of nausea over him as he continued his climb. He forced himself to keep moving, but after a while dizziness claimed him. The whole mountain seemed to be swirling beneath his feet.

Suddenly the injured lawman was on his back, sliding down a grassy slope. He rammed into a tree and lay there, looking toward the whirling sky. His whole body was bathed in sweat, and the nausea grew worse. A black curtain was trying to force its way over his eyes. Rolling his head back and forth, he fought it.

I must not pass out! he gasped to himself. *The cabin . . . I have to get to the cabin . . . to the horse . . . and get away . . .*

The waves of nausea kept coming, but the sheriff willed the black curtain away. His head cleared a little. If he only had some water . . . Then he remembered that he was not far from the stream where he had slaked his thirst when trailing Vic Maynard.

Iron rolled to a sitting position and opened his eyes, blinking against the sharp glare of the sun. Sleeving away sweat from his face, he struggled to his feet and stumbled up the trail once more.

What seemed to him like at least two hours of walking had actually only been twenty minutes when the sparkling stream came into view. Running his tongue around his dry mouth, he hurried toward it, stumbling and falling twice before he reached it.

Iron lay on the bank of the stream, intermittently dipping his face in the cold, clear water and drinking it. Soon his head cleared, the curtain dissolved, and the nausea abated. The water was bringing his strength back.

The rawboned man rose to his feet and looked around. No sign of his pursuers. He was not sure how well he was doing at leaving no sign—though he suspected not well at all, considering he had fallen two times alone in his dash for the stream.

He had taught Vance Maynard well about such things as matted grass. If Maynard came across the spot, he would be breathing down his neck for sure. After bellying down for one more long drink, he limped on. The cabin was not too far away now. Maybe about four miles. One thing, at least, if they caught up to him before he could get away: Only half of them were left. With two guns and plenty of bullets, he might be able to withstand an attack.

*　　*　　*

The other two teams had followed the sound of the last gunshots and simultaneously converged at the bodies of Jess Hall and Yale Chitwood. Vance Maynard was beside himself with anger. He stormed and raged, cursing Iron and swearing to kill him an inch at a time. "I should have tortured and killed him while I had him in my grasp!" he screamed. "This whole scheme has turned sour! This game wasn't supposed to go this way!"

Luke Coffey snarled, "What are *you* so mad about? Four of my men are dead—*my* men. They were my pals. We've been together a long time. And now they're dead . . . dead because of Sheriff Will Iron!"

Chastened, Maynard stopped raging and began to pace around.

Willie Fryar grabbed Coffey's arm. "What do you mean four men are dead?" he demanded. "What happened to Lynch and Whitney?"

"I don't know how he did it, Willie," Coffey muttered, "but he got the drop on 'em and tied 'em to a tree. A grizzly came along and tore 'em both to shreds. Never seen such a bloody sight in all my life."

Harvey Smith looked as if he was going to be sick. "They was ate by a grizzly?" he breathed, his disbelief evident.

To incite anger in Fryar and Smith, Maynard gave them a vivid description of the awful scene. "Iron needs to die, fellas," he told them. "He needs to die real hard and real slow. Let's get moving again. The sooner we find him, the sooner we can get even."

Determined to run the sheriff down, Maynard spread out the two remaining teams and continued the hunt.

Chapter Twelve

The hunted man's progress had been severely hampered by his injured leg, and by dusk Will Iron was still a couple of miles from the Calvert cabin. He leaned against a tree to catch his breath, and pain from his knee coursed through his entire body. Reaching down, he put pressure on the knee, squeezing it with both hands, and even through his pants leg he could feel the heat from the feverish joint. It was badly swollen and throbbing steadily, and it would not take much more of the kind of punishment he was giving it. He had to make it to the cabin . . . and, God willing, the horse.

While waiting for his breathing to become more normal and his heart to stop pounding, he looked up at the sky to gauge how much daylight was left. The glow that remained in the western edge faded as it spread eastward, leaving the rest of the sky a dull gray. Movement caught his eye directly above him, and he looked up to see a lone eagle gliding toward its roost on some rocky crag to wait out the night.

"That's what I need," he said audibly, "a pair of wings."

A wave of dizziness washed over him. He leaned his head against the tree, waiting for the sensation to pass, and for a few moments, silence seemed to descend upon him. As the dizziness gradually subsided, he became aware of the sound of the rising wind, and its whisper in the treetops brought on a feeling of utter solitude. He thought of Vanessa and the children. He was lonesome for them and relished the moment he would see them again.

If you make it, a tiny, needling voice said from somewhere inside his head.

"I'll make it," he said aloud. "I must!"

Iron saw the faint flicker of a few stars. The moon would be full tonight, he knew. He would use its light to reach the cabin.

Pushing away from the tree to continue his journey, the sheriff took a step, and immediately pain stabbed through his knee. He was again assaulted by dizziness and nausea, and his head was beginning to whirl. He was about to pass out when his senses were cleared by the sound of footfalls not too far off and coming his way.

Flattening himself against the tree, he peered around it. Although darkness was quickly closing, he was able to make out another pair of Luke Coffey's men heading directly toward him, guns in their hands. He knew by their slow pace that they had not seen him.

Grimacing against the excruciating pain in his leg, he slipped the revolver from his holster and pulled the other one from under his belt. Carefully and quietly, he thumbed back the hammers. Suddenly another wave of dizziness washed over him. If he passed out now, they would have him!

He fought back and cleared his head. The outlaws drew nearer. Bracing himself, he stepped out from behind the tree, a gun leveled at each man's chest.

Willie Fryar and Harvey Smith jerked with surprise, and Iron's harsh voice commanded, "Hold it right there!"

But Fryar swore and brought his gun up. The weapon in Iron's right hand roared, killing the man instantly. His partner shuddered and tossed down his gun as if it had suddenly turned red-hot. Though tall and muscular and seemingly someone not averse to a good fight, Smith threw his hands over his head and stammered, "D-don't shoot! Please don't shoot!"

Iron was certain the man's meek pose was designed to make him lower his guard. Well, the outlaw had another guess coming. He kept his right-hand gun trained on Smith while sliding the other one under his belt. Although he was struggling against a fuzzy brain once again, he masked it by glaring at Smith and lining up the muzzle between the man's eyes. His voice was filled with scorn as he rasped, "You having fun with your little game? Looks like it's my move now!"

Smith's raised hands were trembling as he said weakly, "Please, Sheriff, don't kill me! I really didn't want in on this, but I had no choice! Honest! Luke said I had to cooperate or they'd kill me, too."

"Shut up, you sniveling liar!" Iron snapped. "Besides, I'm not interested in killing you—unless you force me to. I'm going to tie you to one of these trees and keep moving."

Smith's face turned white—and this time his fear did not appear to be an act. "No! Please!" he gasped. "You tied Norm and Ted to trees, and a grizzly tore 'em to shreds!"

Iron was shocked to learn of it but felt no sympathy for the two men. Their way of life had led them to their untimely death. Waving the gun at Smith, he muttered, "Just as you didn't have a choice, I don't have one, either. Back up to that tree and put your arms around it behind you."

Reluctantly, the outlaw obeyed.

Iron battled the dizziness that threatened to overcome him and held his gun on Smith as the trembling man backed up against the tree. He yanked a red-and-white, polka-dotted bandanna out of the outlaw's back pocket and said, "I'm obliged to you for providing me with this. You make one false move while I'm tying your hands and this'll be your day to shake hands with the devil."

The lawman took a step and landed awkwardly on the uneven ground. A fresh spiral of pain shot through his knee, and his teeth clicked as he snapped his mouth shut and groaned. His legs suddenly turned watery and dizziness sapped him. He stagged backward two steps, dropping the bandanna and raising his hand to his temple.

Smith quickly pulled away from the tree and started toward him. The gun in Iron's hand felt as though it weighed a hundred pounds. Swaying, he could barely raise the weapon as he warned in a slurred voice, "Don't you move, mister! I'll—"

The earth seemed to open up under Iron's unsteady feet. He felt the gun slip from his fingers just before darkness swallowed him up.

Harvey Smith threw his head back and laughed heartily. The outlaw bent down and yanked the revolver from under Iron's belt, then picked up the other one. Chortling gleefully, he stood over the unconscious sheriff and said, "Looks like the shoe's on the other foot, don't it, lawman?"

Picking up his own gun, he fired it once and then twice again—the agreed-upon signal. That done, he grabbed his bandanna from Iron's fingers and used it to tie the sheriff's hands behind his back. Figuring enough time had passed, he fired the signal again.

He repeated the signal at regular intervals. Soon it was so dark that Smith could not see his hand in front of his face. "Come on, you guys," he muttered. "Where are you?"

Presently, the full moon appeared over the peaks to the east, clear and bright against the inky blackness of the night, and dully lit the landscape around him. Smith glanced down at the still-unconscious lawman and snarled, "It won't be long now 'fore Vance Maynard gives you what you got comin'. Come to think of it, there ain't no reason why I shouldn't give you a little taste beforehand, now is there?"

Chuckling evilly, he sent a swift kick to Iron's rib cage. The lawman groaned but showed no sign of coming around. The outlaw fired off three more shots, then leaned over the prostrate sheriff, glaring at him. "If it wasn't for the money I got comin', I'd kill you myself, for what you did to Willie and seein' as how you'd likely've left me tied to that tree to die. Well, *you're* the one's gonna die—and I'm gonna be rich."

Several more minutes passed before Vance Maynard and Luke Coffey finally reached their cohort. As they drew up and saw the unconscious Will Iron, Coffey grinned at Smith. "Well, I declare!"

Maynard clapped Smith on the back and shouted, "Whooee! You did it, Harvey! You did it! Where's Willie? In the bushes relieving himself?"

Smith's face grew grim. "Willie's dead." He nodded at the body lying several feet away, barely visible in the shadows, and said, "Iron killed him."

Coffey shot a look of hatred at Iron, then looked back at Smith. "So how'd you get the drop on him?"

Wanting to look good in his cronies' eyes, the owlhoot thought fast, then replied, "Well, while Iron was cuttin' Willie down, I got the drop on him, then smashed him one on the jaw. He went down like I'd clubbed him. I tied him up real quick, and there he is."

Maynard knelt beside Iron and started slapping his face. "Come on, Sheriff!" he shouted. "Wake up! I can't play the game I've got in mind for you if you're not awake to enjoy it!"

When Iron did not stir, Maynard looked at Smith and asked, "How long since you coldcocked him?"

The outlaw rubbed his bearded chin. "Well, I'm not exactly sure."

Shaking his head, Maynard muttered, "Most likely he passed out all by himself from pain."

Smith bristled. "You callin' me a liar?" he demanded, his tone menacing, as he walked stiffly toward Maynard.

Maynard smirked. "Yeah, that's exactly what I'm doing. I've seen Iron in action. There's no way you could best him in a draw."

Smith's hand started for his gun, but Luke Coffey leapt between the men. Facing his cohort, he put his hands on Smith's shoulders. "That's enough, Harv!" he snapped. "Now, you just cool down!" Turning, he told Maynard, "And I'd advise *you* not to make enemies of fellas you need. Fact is, it don't matter none how Iron got unconscious, just that he is. So I suggest we just settle down over there on them logs and take a breather for ourselves till he comes 'round."

The others nodded in agreement, and the threesome sat down on fallen trunks. Harvey Smith, sitting by himself, was sullen and quiet, but Maynard and Coffey were highly animated as they sat side by side, swapping ideas on how to best get revenge on Sheriff Will Iron.

Unbeknownst to any of them, Will Iron came to. He was first aware of the nearby voices. Then, as his senses returned, he realized his hands were bound and quickly figured out what had happened. But though he was clearly in a terrible predicament, there was very little pain in his bad leg. In fact, it felt numb.

Iron moved his head slightly, giving him a view of all three men. The one he had started to tie to a tree was quiet. It was Maynard and Coffey who were talking. The lawman lay there, unmoving, trying to figure a way to free his hands and escape. Suddenly, the quiet one stood up. Iron closed his eyes and lay still.

Smith stepped to Maynard and stood over him. He

broke into the others' conversation, saying, "I been thinkin'. Since my partner ain't alive to collect for his part in findin' Iron, I want his share, too."

Maynard rose to his feet and met Smith's cold gaze. "I don't see it that way, Smith. You hardly deserve the thousand, since you·didn't capture Iron; he passed out. You sure aren't gonna get two thousand."

Smith bristled. "That ain't fair, Maynard!" he blared. "No matter how it happened, the fact is, when you and Luke got here, Iron was tied up and helpless, just like you ordered. Me and Willie did our job. You owe the team the full bonus, and I aim to collect it!"

Maynard laughed harshly. "Well, your aim is off, mister! Fryar's dead, and his share of the bonus died when he did. Now, you better shut up about it, or I'm likely to change my mind and not give you one stinking dollar!"

Smith's eyes narrowed, and his muscular body seemed to swell with his anger. Whipping out his gun, he pointed it at Maynard and snapped, "I smell a dirty skunk lookin' for a way to back out on a deal, Maynard! Your prey is lyin' there tied up, and I'm the one who tied him!" Shaking the gun at Maynard, Smith bellowed, "We're goin' to town first thing in the mornin', and I'm gettin' my two thousand!" Smith shifted his fiery gaze to his boss and demanded, "Go on, Luke. Tell him I'm right."

But Coffey said instead, "Put the gun away, Harv. Vance is one of our own kind. You shouldn't be actin' this way toward him. Just simmer down. That thousand-dollar bonus is fair enough."

Smith scowled at Coffey and rasped, "I can't believe what I'm hearin'! What's the matter with you? Are you lettin' this cheatin' four-flusher win you over?"

Coffey scowled back. "I said put the gun away, Harvey. You're actin' like an idiot."

"Yeah," Maynard interjected, smirking, "an idiot that won't get a wooden nickel now."

Smith was furious. Spittle appeared at the corners of his mouth and his gun hand trembled from having to control his rage. "You're guaranteein' me two thousand when we get to town, right now . . . or else!"

Calmly, Luke Coffey reached toward Smith, ordering, "Give me the gun, Harvey. This has gone far enough."

Smith took a step back. "You tell him to make me that promise, Luke! If he don't, I'll kill him here and now!"

Coffey's voice was threatening as he held out his hand and repeated, "Give me the gun, Harvey!"

Smith went blind with fury at being betrayed. Turning his gun on Coffey, he pulled the trigger. As his boss fell, the enraged outlaw brought the gun around toward Maynard, but Smith had underestimated the man's speed on the draw. Maynard's gun was out and aimed straight at Smith's heart. The gun boomed. Smith jerked from the impact, then winced, dropping his weapon. Clutching his chest, he staggered a few steps, his face filled with disbelief, then collapsed.

With the smoking gun still in his hand, Maynard leaned over Smith and felt for a pulse at the side of his neck. There was none. Stepping to Coffey, he knelt beside him and saw that he had been gut-shot. Coffey was gripping his abdomen, blood oozing between his fingers. It was evident that he was dying. Squeezing his shoulder, Maynard said, "I sure do appreciate you trying to talk sense into that idiot. I didn't figure he'd shoot you. I'm sorry I wasn't able to plug him before he shot you."

The mortally wounded man coughed, then mumbled, "He dead?"

"Yeah."

Coffey jerked with a spasm of pain. "Guess my gang's gone, Vance."

Nodding, Maynard removed his jacket and rolled it up, then slipped it under Coffey's head. "Here. This'll make you a bit more comfortable. I'm real sorry things turned out this way." He gently patted the outlaw's shoulder. "I gotta check on Iron. Be back in a minute."

He turned and hurried over to where Iron had been lying, then drew up short. His prisoner was gone. Cursing the lawman vehemently, Maynard drew his gun, then picked up Smith's revolver and, both guns cocked and ready to fire, searched the area. Iron's hands had been bound and he was unarmed. It should not be too hard to recapture him.

Suddenly a large bank of clouds drifted over the moon, plunging the forest into near darkness. Swearing at the rotten timing, Maynard cautiously made his way back to Luke Coffey and knelt beside him. He spoke softly to him, but there was no reply. The outlaw leader was dead.

Swearing again, Maynard sat down on the ground and leaned against a tree. He would have to wait till morning to begin trailing his father's killer.

Will Iron moved through the timber as fast as he could in the darkness. The heated argument had been just the distraction he had needed to slip away. He had paused briefly when the shots were fired, thinking at first that they were meant for him. But then he had realized that they were the end result of the fight. He assumed somebody had been killed. He had a strong feeling that it was not Vance Maynard. He wished for a gun himself.

Iron's leg was completely numb, and he was forced to drag it. He knew he was leaving a trail that even an amateur could follow, but there was nothing else he could do. Once he was a safe distance away, he took time to free his hands by rubbing the bandanna in two against the rough bark of a tree, then started off again.

He paused when the moonlight was mostly blotted out by a cloud mass; however, enough ambient light remained for him to continue on cautiously. He had the advantage over Maynard now. Whereas he had a good enough idea as to where he was heading to be able to make his way even by night, his pursuer needed light to be able to follow his trail. Iron found himself a sturdy branch—a fine walking stick—and used it to help make his way through the night. Again he thought of the obvious trail he was leaving, but he told himself it did not matter. He would reach the Calvert cabin and, with luck, the bay mare, hours ahead of Vance Maynard. Then he would have won the game.

After a couple of hours he heard flowing water. Following the sound, he found a bubbling spring and, sighing gratefully, scooped up handful after handful of the cold water, drinking till his thirst was slaked. He then splashed his face with the cool, soothing water.

Feeling refreshed, the lawman took up his slow travel once again. The bad leg was beginning to tingle, and the pain that the numbness had dulled was making itself known again.

He continued on for some three more hours. The clouds had dissipated, and the moon was again shining brightly. It was lowering in the western sky when Iron spotted the Calvert cabin no more than a hundred yards away. Drawing up and leaning against a tree, he studied first the cabin and then the adjoining pasture. The bay mare was nowhere in sight. His heart sank. Without the horse, he was done for.

Suddenly a spasm of new, excruciating pain tore at his knee. Gripping the tree trunk, he looked down at the swelling that pressed against his pants leg. What was happening to it now? The horrible spasm was immediately followed by an oceanlike wave of dizziness too strong for him to fight off. Sliding down the side of the tree, he slumped against the base of the trunk and passed out.

Vance Maynard had fallen asleep, knowing he could not take up his pursuit until he had more light. The chirping of birds in the trees awoke him, and he sat up sharply to find dawn breaking in the east. Rising from the hard ground, he looked around at the three dead outlaws and smiled. He had fared quite well, he thought. Luke Coffey and his men had helped locate Iron—and he wouldn't have to put out a dollar.

Scouting the area, it took the vengeful hunter only minutes to pick up the injured lawman's trail. It was obvious he was dragging his bad leg. Maynard chuckled to himself. Tracking Iron from here on in was going to be a cinch.

He visualized what he would do when he got his hands on the man who had forced his father into suicide. Hatred for Iron roiled up in him. Picking up his pace until he was almost running through the forest, he breathed aloud, "I'm gonna hunt you down just like you did my dad, Iron! I *will* have my pound of flesh!"

Chapter Thirteen

The branches scratched Will Iron's face and tore at his clothes. The forest floor was covered with a thick fog, hiding the huge roots that tripped him with every step. Suddenly, standing before him with red, demonic eyes was Vance Maynard, a cocked revolver in each hand. "You should have let my father go, Will Iron! He leapt into the canyon because you made him do it! *You*, Will Iron, *you* made him do it!"

"No!" Iron screamed. "No, you're wrong!"

A malignant gleam of triumph flashed in Maynard's eyes as he hissed, "You can't get away from me, Sheriff! You made my father take his own life. Now I am going to make you take yours!"

Iron took a fearful step backward. Like a finger of the dead, the hanging branch of a tree brushed the skin on his face.

Maynard threw his head back and laughed victoriously. "You can't get away from me, Iron! Come on—it's time to pay the piper!"

Abruptly, the injured lawman whirled and ran, dragging his lame leg. Maynard's heinous laughter seemed to surround him. Then suddenly Maynard was in front of him, grinning evilly, pointing his revolvers directly at Iron's chest. "No!" Iron screamed, trying to outrun the man. But it was useless.

Suddenly Iron's eyes flew open, and the sun's rays stabbed them painfully. He found himself sitting beside a tree in the middle of the Rocky Mountain forest. His entire body was bathed in sweat. His heart was pounding. "It was a dream!" he gasped.

The effects of the nightmare hung on as Iron, using his makeshift walking stick, struggled to his feet. Shuffling toward the Calvert cabin, he muttered, "You aren't going to get me, Maynard. I'm going to live through this ordeal. Somehow I'll work my way out of this and see you face a judge and jury."

As he neared the cabin, Iron was elated to see the bay mare standing near the corral gate, watching his progress. He almost shouted with joy. She must have been in the barn when he had first looked earlier. A quick glance behind him showed no sign of pursuers. He would saddle the mare and ride hard for Casper, taking a different route from the one he had come by. He would be holding Vanessa and the kids in his arms by sundown.

Suddenly Iron heard a wild uproar of barking, growling, and snapping of fierce jaws. Off to his right, by the pond at the edge of the clearing, he saw a pack of wild dogs tearing apart a large beaver. Iron's mouth went dry. The dogs had not noticed him yet. If they did . . . He glanced toward the cabin. Though it was barely more than forty yards away, it suddenly seemed like a mile, but he had to reach it. Iron knew about wild dogs in these mountains. Wolves feared human beings and would not attack a man unless they were cornered or rabid, but wild dogs *would* attack. The lawman knew of many instances in the past few years of wild dogs killing and eating hunters and trappers.

As the beasts fought among themselves, snarling and snapping as each dog attempted to keep its share from the others, the sheriff hobbled toward the cabin, dragging his bad leg. Keeping his eyes riveted on the dogs, he backed his way toward the cabin. His tense breathing began to ease as he drew near the porch. *Just a few more yards,* he told himself. *Just a few more yards . . .*

All of a sudden one of the dogs lifted its head, blood dripping from its slavering jowls, and looked at Iron. The lawman's blood froze. The rest of the pack then looked his way, and in unison they decided to attack. They took off after him, barking and growling, eyes wild and fangs bared. As he lurched toward the cabin, Iron fell, dropping the walking stick. Panic raced through him. Breathing hard, he gained his feet and stumbled on, dragging his useless leg.

Will Iron had faced death more times than he could remember. Many an evil-eyed man had tried to put him in his grave. He had even faced down four and five men at a time and come out the victor. But this was different. If he did not make it into the cabin and get the door closed, he would be torn to bits.

He had just reached the porch when he fell again. Crying out, he crawled madly across the rough floorboards toward the door, gasping for air. The hellish hounds were bearing down rapidly, growling and snapping their teeth, saliva and blood glistening on their ragged coats. Gripping the doorknob, Iron used it to pull himself erect, then turned it.

The door opened and the lawman dashed inside, hurriedly pivoting to close the door. But before he could close it completely, the attacking dogs hit it with tremendous force. Iron stumbled to the side as the snarling hounds bowled through, one on top of the other. It would only be seconds before they got unscrambled and came after him.

He looked quickly around, then lunged for the ladder that led up to the loft. Grabbing a rung, he started hauling himself up, but two dogs were suddenly below him. They repeatedly leapt up at him, like crazed marionettes whose strings were being jerked. One caught hold of the lawman's pants leg and slashed it with its fangs but fortunately missed the flesh. As it dropped back to the floor, the other dog pincered the heel of Iron's left boot. The pressure of the hound's jaws was tremendous, but the thick heel and boot leather kept the fangs from penetrating through to his foot.

The animal hung on. Iron gripped the rung and kicked the dog's face with his other foot. It took three blows, but the dog finally let go and fell on top of a couple of others.

Two more replaced the first ones. The smaller of them started to tentatively climb the rungs, but it lost its momentum and slid down. With a yelp it landed hard on its back. The harried lawman was about to push himself over the edge of the loft when the largest dog in the pack bounded off the floor over the others. It sailed upward, its powerful jaws snapping violently. Hanging on to the top rung, Iron kicked the dog in the head with all his might. The dog went down, taking several others with it, and hit the floor, stunned.

The lawman finally managed to haul himself onto the floor of the loft. The wild dogs yapped and snarled as they continued to try to reach their prey. Iron lay on his back, sweat pouring from his face. The din created by the savage hounds thundered in his ears. He rolled over and looked down at them. Their blood-splattered coats were dull, and their ribs showed starkly through them. They no doubt had been short on food for some time. They were eager to kill and eat anything or anyone they could corner. Breathing hard, he counted seven of them.

While the wild din continued, Iron came up with a plan. He figured if he could find a way to close the door and pen up the dogs in the house, he could escape through the window that led from the loft onto the porch roof. But he had to do it quickly, then bridle and saddle the bay mare and ride away before Vance Maynard and whoever else was left could find him.

Looking around for something to use to close the door, which was immediately below the edge of the loft, Iron spied a broom lying in a corner of the loft. He limped over to it and grabbed it, then crawled back to the edge and looked down. Gripping the broom just below the straw bristles, he lowered it, placing the tip of the handle against the open door. When he did, the dogs congregated at the door, leaping up and snapping at the broomstick. Their bodies blocked the door, and he could not close it.

Cursing, Iron pulled the broom back to the loft. Somehow he had to get the ravenous beasts away from the door. Then his eye caught the bowl of hardtack, still sitting where he had left it on top of the cupboard. The dogs were so hungry they would no doubt pounce on anything edible. Could he reach it? He was not sure. Using the broom once more, he leaned out over the edge of the loft. Maddeningly, his reach fell about a half-foot shy of the target. He groaned inwardly.

He looked around the loft. There was nothing else that he could use.

"Think, Will!" he commanded himself. His boot! He quickly removed his right boot and hung it off the end of the broom handle. He then scurried to the edge of the loft and tried again. It fell an inch or so too short. He pulled back the broom and adjusted the boot, hanging it farther out. This time it reached. Using the toe of the boot, he knocked the bowl to the floor. Instantly, the dogs dived into the hardtack and began gulping it down.

Iron quickly put his boot back on. With the hounds occupied, the sheriff was able to push the door shut with the broom, hard enough for it to latch. Breathing a sigh of relief, he hurried to the window, slid the bolt that locked it, and swung it open. Now he could slip through the window, drop off the porch roof, and get away on the horse. In just a few hours he would be back with his family.

He froze in his tracks. Just as he was about to go through the window, he saw a man emerging from the shadows of the timber and running toward the cabin. It was Vance Maynard.

Iron's stomach lurched. For a moment he was absolutely motionless, as if he had been hypnotized. Maynard was coming with a gun in each hand . . . and Iron was unarmed. His mind raced. What could he do? Beneath him were the vicious wild dogs, and coming for him with vengeance blazing in his eyes was a well-armed man intent on killing him.

Vance Maynard suddenly spotted the lawman looking through the window and skidded to a halt. Laughing fiendishly, he called, "Hey, Sheriff, couldn't you find a better place to hide than that? What's the matter? Is that old leg of yours keeping you from getting away?"

Maynard was clearly feeling a surge of elation. He had his man cornered, and he knew Iron was unarmed. Taunting him, Maynard chuckled and declared, "Too bad you don't have any weapons, Sheriff! That sorta leaves me holding the trump card, doesn't it?" His expression abruptly changed, and he blared, "I could blast you from where I stand, but if I did that, you'd die much too easy! You're gonna suffer, mister! I owe you for what you did to my dad!" As he spoke Vance Maynard bolted for the cabin.

Up in the loft the lawman figured that from the way Maynard was rushing toward the cabin, he was obviously so intent on issuing justice to Will Iron that he did not notice the footprints of the dogs in the soft earth by the porch. And since the ravenous animals were busy wolfing down the hardtack, they were quiet and would not announce their presence.

Iron knew what Maynard was about to face, but he did not call out a warning. It was clear that the man could not be reasoned with—he was far too bent on exacting revenge to listen to reason—and since Iron was unarmed, he had no other choice but to let Vance Maynard meet his fate.

Without breaking stride, holding both guns ready, Maynard thundered across the porch and kicked open the door. The muscular man's thrust broke the latch, and the door flew open. Grinning evilly, Maynard charged inside.

The savage dogs whipped their heads up at the sudden intrusion, eyes blazing and fangs showing. Maynard's grin disappeared instantly. His face went white and his mouth fell open.

Instantly the hungry hounds sprang toward Maynard, snarling and snapping ferociously. He started to bring the guns up, but it was too late. The impact of the dogs hitting him knocked him down. Sharp teeth slashed at his face and ripped at his clothing. Kicking and elbowing at the beasts, he managed to hang onto the guns and scramble to his feet, but one of the dogs snapped its powerful jaws around the hunter's left hand, piercing it deeply with its fangs. The hand was now useless.

Blood ran into Maynard's eyes, almost blinding him. A big dog leapt at him, its mouth wide open and fangs snapping. Maynard managed to shove the barrel of his gun into its throat and pull the trigger. The report sounded like a cannon in the close quarters as the slug tore through the dog's head.

The sound of the shot stunned the pack for a few seconds, but then they went at the man again. Vance

Maynard screamed as he went down under the attack of the remaining six vicious, snapping balls of fur. He kicked and writhed in a desperate attempt to stave off his attackers, and at one point he looked up—at the face of Will Iron.

Looking into his enemy's eyes, Maynard screamed, "Iron! Do something! Iron, they'll kill me! Help me! Get them off me!"

But Iron did nothing as the wild beasts tore Maynard to shreds.

While the dogs feasted on Vance Maynard's corpse, Iron crawled out onto the roof of the porch, then dropped to the ground, managing to land on his good leg. He stumbled but quickly regained his balance and limped to the barn. The bay mare had fled from sight at the arrival of the dogs, but Iron hoped she had sought shelter in the barn.

She was there. Grabbing a saddle and bridle, he talked to her soothingly. She seemed pleased at having human companionship and walked over to him. "Come on, girl!" he called softly. "That's it."

She stood patiently while he quickly saddled and bridled her. Unable to put his left leg in the stirrup, he gripped the saddle horn and hoisted himself slowly into the saddle. Lifting his hat and wiping sweat from his brow with his sleeve, he said, "Okay, girl, take me home."

Chapter Fourteen

Outlaw Albert Norberg was waiting with the horses, pacing like a caged lion. Periodically casting a glance toward the west, Norberg swore aloud, impatient for the others to appear. Had something happened to the gang and to Vance Maynard? It should not have taken this long to hunt down a limping man.

As the morning wore on, the outlaw decided to have some breakfast. After building a small campfire and filling the coffeepot from a small stream nearby, he pulled out some hardtack, then sat back and waited for the coffee to brew. While he ate, he kept an eye on the foothills to the west. Surely Luke and the others would show up soon. What could be keeping them?

When Norberg had taken his fill, he rinsed out the coffeepot and put it back in Hall's sack. Rolling himself a cigarette, he lit it and began pacing again. The outlaw wondered if perhaps his cronies had been tracked down by a posse and were in the hands of the law. Shaking his head, he told himself that if that were the case, the posse would have come after him, too.

To the forefront of his mind came Sheriff Will Iron. Norberg had heard many tales about the indomitable sheriff of Natrona County, Wyoming. Could Iron somehow have found a way to take out each of the gang members and Vance Maynard? "No!" he exclaimed aloud. "There ain't no way! The man's got a bad leg . . . and

he was turned loose in those mountains totally unarmed. There's no way he could have—"

Norberg's soliloquy was cut short when he spotted a
lone rider on a bay horse heading his way. He decided
it was some local rancher going somewhere. After all,
Luke and the boys were all on foot.

Moments later the outlaw tensed. As the rider drew
closer, Norberg could make out his light gray hat—and
the man's left leg was extended forward stiffly. It was
Sheriff Iron!

Cold sweat formed on Norberg's brow, and he twitched
as if an icicle had been stuck down the back of his shirt.
Wheeling, he dashed for his horse. Iron was returning,
but there was no sign of the others. What had happened to them? Had the legendary lawman actually
overcome them? Were they dead?

Albert Norberg was not going to wait to find out.
Fear gripping his heart, he leapt into his saddle and
spurred his horse, plunging into the woods before Iron
could catch sight of him.

As Will Iron rode the bay mare down out of the
foothills, the pain in his injured leg increased. The only
way he could stand it at all was to keep his left foot out
of the stirrup and to hold the leg stiffly up.

Nearing the plains, the lawman noticed a cluster of
horses tied to some aspens near a small stream. Drawing closer, he recognized the animals as those belonging to the Luke Coffey gang. Albert Norberg was gone.
Needing a few minutes out of the saddle anyway, Iron
eased himself to the ground and limped to the horses,
telling them, "Can't leave you here like this, can I?"

He removed their saddles, dropping them to the
ground. He then took off their bridles and freed them
from the trees. Before traveling on, he dug into Jess
Hall's canvas sack and found some beef jerky. Then he
started to remount. But his head began to spin, bring-

ing nausea with it, and he could feel himself starting to pass out. Forcing himself to stay conscious, he limped to the stream and plunged his face into the cold water. The water revived him, and he returned to the mare.

But his strength was waning, and it took several minutes to get back into the saddle. Once mounted, he clucked softly to the mare and headed the horse across the prairie toward Casper.

As he rode for home, enduring the pain, Iron wondered what would happen to the knee. Was there anything left of the joint? Something was wrong in there —real wrong. If he lost the use of his leg, he would not be able to take any of the jobs offered by the ranchers. It would hinder him in getting other kinds of jobs, too. What would the future hold for an ex-lawman who had only one good leg? How would he make a living and provide for his family?

One thing Will Iron knew: Whatever the future held and no matter how tough things might get, Vanessa would stand by him. The woman had grit. And she loved her husband—as much as he loved her. Trying to look on the bright side, Iron told himself that as long as he had Vanessa and his kids, he would make it, no matter what happened.

The sun was low in the sky when the lawman reached the familiar hills and gullies he knew like the back of his hand. Having angled in from the mountains, he reached the road leading into Casper at a point about ten miles from home.

Horse and rider soon topped a hill, and there ahead of him Iron saw his town. It almost seemed as though it were a mirage, after what he had gone through the last two days. He told himself that home had never looked so good.

Suddenly, spasms of pain began to shoot through his knee and course through his body. Nausea claimed him, and dizziness made his head spin. The animal he was on seemed to be swaying and bobbing like a small boat on a stormy sea. Bending low and gripping the saddle horn, Iron fought hard to stay conscious. But the dizziness grew worse, and the nausea increased. Knowing he was going to pass out, he tried to dismount before he fell from the horse. He was halfway off the mare when he lost consciousness and fell to the ground in a heap.

He had lain there for an hour when a rancher and his wife came along in their buckboard and spotted the horse standing in the middle of the road. Touching her husband's arm, the woman said, "Someone's lying beside that horse!"

Snapping the reins, the rancher called, "Git up there!"

Moments later, the buckboard came to a quick halt and the rancher hopped down, hurrying to the crumpled form that lay in the dusty road. He took one look at the unconscious man and called to his wife, "It's Will Iron! Come give me a hand! We've got to get him to Doc Boulder!"

The woman hoisted her skirts and climbed down from the buckboard.

Together they hauled Will Iron's limp form to the wagon and placed him gently in the back. Then they tied the bay mare to the tailgate, climbed back onto the seat, and put the team to a gallop.

Will Iron came to and found himself lying on a bed in the clinic. As he blinked to clear his vision, he heard a soft, familiar voice say, "He's coming around, Doctor."

Looking toward the voice, he saw Vanessa standing over him. "Welcome back, darling," she told him, smiling through tears.

Running his tongue over dry lips, he asked, "How . . . how did I get here?"

"A couple picked you up on the road about nine

miles west. I'll tell you all about it later. Here. Let's get some water in you."

Vanessa lifted her husband's head with one hand and held a cup to his lips with the other. Dr. Joel Boulder nodded encouragingly. "Go ahead and drain the cup, Will. It'll do you good."

When the cup was empty, Iron looked at his wife and asked tenderly, "You all right?"

"Yes," the redhead assured him, "now that you're back." She kissed him, then stroked his brow.

"Where are the kids?"

Vanessa smiled. "Right over here."

She motioned to Joshua and Amanda, who quickly rushed over and hugged their father.

The physician looked down at the lawman, his face grim. Clearing his throat, he said, "Will, I had to operate on the knee again. It was necessary to remove what was left of the joint, or eventually I'd have had to amputate the whole leg." He hesitated, then continued, "I'm afraid you'll never bend that leg again. Without the knee joint, you'll walk stiff-legged for the rest of your life." Vanessa clutched Iron's hand as the doctor continued, "You'll be on crutches for quite a while, then you'll graduate to a cane. Only after many long months will you be able to walk without a cane."

Boulder patted his shoulder. "I'm sorry, Will, but your days as a lawman are definitely over. This time you must turn in your badge and hang up your gun for good."

"Guess I knew that before I got here," Iron replied tonelessly. He looked at Vanessa, who was crying soundlessly. She wiped the tears from her eyes and squeezed her husband's hand reassuringly.

"Will," Boulder said, "there are some others out in the waiting room who'd like to see you. Are you up to having visitors?"

"I'm okay," Iron replied. "Send them in."

Boulder went to the door. "All right, gentlemen," he called, "you may come in. I'll give you fifteen minutes and then he'll have to rest."

Iron turned his head and saw Jim Stenzel walk through the door. Behind him came council chairman Ty Miller, followed by the entire town council. Vanessa and the children stepped back, allowing the men to surround the bed.

Grinning up at his faithful friend, Iron asked Stenzel, "How are you feeling, ol' pal?"

"Doc says I'm recovering even better than he expected," Stenzel replied. "How did you injure your knee again? Did you catch those two killers? What happened to Jack Lancaster?"

The lawman shook his head. "It's a long story, but the two killers are dead. So is Jack Lancaster . . . only Jack Lancaster wasn't Jack Lancaster."

Stenzel's face was a picture of confusion. "Huh?"

Iron explained the whole story to his visitors, including the treachery of the impostor and of the man's horrible death. When Iron had finished, everyone stood stunned for a long moment. Then Ty Miller motioned for Vanessa and the children to come close, and they drew up. The redhead took hold of her husband's hand and smiled, already knowing what was coming.

Miller said, "Will, as soon as you rode out of town in pursuit of those two killers, I called a meeting of the council. I announced to these men that it was time I stepped aside as council chairman and allowed the town to elect a mayor. Casper is on the grow, as is my own thriving business, which I need to look after. I knew you'd have to return to your retirement when you came back from your pursuit, so I talked to Vanessa about this mayor idea, and she liked it."

He paused and looked at the redhead, who was smiling proudly at her husband. Proceeding, Miller said, "I then called a town meeting and made two proposals:

one, that we create the office of mayor, and two, that we cast a vote on the spot for the man we wanted. My ideas were unanimously approved of—and *you* were elected."

Iron grinned. "Without even putting my hat in the ring?"

"Yep. The people have spoken. Your salary will begin at a hundred dollars a month more than you were being paid as county sheriff. If you will accept it, the job is yours."

Iron looked up at his wife. Tears were streaming down her cheeks. Squeezing her small, soft hand, he looked at Miller and said in a voice filled with emotion, "I'll take the job."

He then reached down and removed the sheriff's badge from his shirt. Handing it to Jim Stenzel, he said, "I know you'll wear this badge as proudly as I did, Jim, so I feel good about giving it up. I wore a badge for so many years that I never thought about doing anything else. But I guess, like it says in Ecclesiastes, there's a time for everything—and that means there's an end to things, too."

Will Iron was sworn in as mayor of Casper, Wyoming, then and there. While his children clapped their hands with glee and the rest of the group joined them, Vanessa leaned close to her husband and said softly, "I've never kissed a mayor before."

The handsome, rawboned ex-lawman grinned and replied, "Give it a try and see if you like it."

After a long, tender kiss, the beautiful woman stood erect and smiled down at her husband.

"Well?" he asked.

She leaned close once more. "Mm-hmm," she whispered. "I like it."

And she kissed him again.

If you enjoyed this book, look for the bold new series from Bantam and Book Creations. . . .

CODY'S LAW

Featuring Sam Cody, Texas Ranger

Now available at your bookstore . . .
Book 1: *Gunmetal Justice*
Book 2: *Die Lonesome*

For an exciting preview of Book 3, *Border Showdown,* to be published in December 1991, turn the page. . . .

The trouble with routine patrols, Cody thought, was that they were just that—routine. He and his fellow Rangers, Seth Williams and Alan Northrup, had been riding the plains of the border country around Del Rio, Texas, for three days and hadn't run into any outlaws or renegade Indians or seen one sign of trouble. Despite that, Cody knew all too well that lawlessness had been on the rise lately; Captain Wallace Vickery, the commanding officer of Ranger Company C, had taken to pounding his fist on his desk and shouting that something had to be done about the influx of killers and holdup artists and wide loopers in the area. That was why Cody and his two young partners were out on patrol.

Problem was, he mused, you couldn't do anything about outlaws if you couldn't find 'em.

Cody pulled his rangy lineback dun to a halt at the top of a slight rise and took off his dark brown Stetson. Sleeving sweat from his forehead, he looked over at his companions, who had come to a halt beside him, and said, "I reckon we might as well head back to Del Rio. Looks like all the owlhoots've gone off to visit the prairie dogs."

"He means they're all holed up," Seth said to Alan.

"I know what he means," Alan snapped. "You don't have to explain it to me."

"Don't start getting proddy," Cody told them. "It's still a long, hot ride back to Del Rio. Best save your grousing for later." Del Rio was some five miles to the southwest, and if Cody looked hard enough, he could see the narrow strip of green on the horizon that marked the course of the Rio Grande.

"Well, it's not getting any cooler just sitting here," Cody said. "We might as well head on in." He heeled his horse into a ground-eating trot, and Seth and Alan fell in beside him.

The three Rangers had been riding for another ten minutes or so when Cody suddenly reined in. "Hold on," he called to his companions. "Listen to that."

Alan frowned and asked, "Listen to what?"

"No, wait a minute! I hear it, too," Seth said, excitement growing in his voice. "Those are gunshots!"

Cody nodded curtly as the sound of distant firing grew more constant. "Somebody's burning a lot of powder," he said. "Let's go see what it's all about!"

The crackling of gunshots grew louder as the three Rangers rode through a shallow valley and then up another rise. As they crested the top of the slope, Cody's sharp eyes immediately took in the scene being played out below them. A narrow road wandered along about two hundred yards away, and just to one side of it lay an overturned wagon. One of the horses in its team was down on the ground, lying motionless and probably dead. The other horses had managed to thrash their way back to their feet, but they couldn't go anywhere because they were still attached to the wagon. They danced around nervously as gunfire crashed.

Several people had taken cover behind the wagon, and though they were too far away for Cody to determine how many of them there were, he was certain there was at least one woman among the group. They were sporadically returning the fire of a group of men mounted on horseback who were riding back and forth in front of the wagon and sniping at it with rifles.

Cody flung up a hand, signaling the other Rangers to halt, and reached into his saddlebags. As he did so,

Seth burst out, "Aren't we going to go help those folks, Cody?"

"Never hurts to find out for sure what the situation is before you go charging in—especially when there's lead flying around," Cody said, taking out a pair of field glasses. Focusing the lenses on the riders, he studied the men for a moment, then grunted. "Yep, I recognize a couple of those hombres. Nate Vaughn and Ben Sherman. They're wanted in every county from here to Bexar."

Seth unsheathed his Winchester. "Then let's go get 'em before those innocent folks get hurt." Alan was reaching for his rifle, too.

Cody nodded and stowed the field glasses away. As he slid his Winchester from the saddle boot, he heeled the dun into motion again. "Make your shots count, boys!" he called as the horse galloped down the hill.

The back of a running horse was no kind of platform to shoot from with any kind of accuracy, and putting a bullet in the general vicinity of what you aimed at was damned good, Cody knew. He didn't fire until he judged that he and the other Rangers had come within rifle range, and then he reined in and brought the dun to a halt before he lifted the Winchester to his shoulder. The horse was used to sudden, loud noises, and it stood steady as Cody lined his sights on one of the raiders and squeezed the trigger. The man flung his arms up and started to slide out of the saddle, catching the horn at the last moment and hanging on desperately.

Beside Cody, Seth and Alan had also brought their mounts to a stop, and their rifles cracked as they opened up on their targets. The bandits ducked instinctively as lead whined around their heads, though one of them slumped over in his saddle. It was impossible to tell whose bullet had hit him—whether one of the Rangers' or one of the defenders'—but that didn't matter. The outlaws were milling around in confusion now, their plan to rob the wagon shot to hell by this unexpected attack.

A couple of them threw slugs toward the Rangers, but the shots didn't come anywhere close. And then suddenly the raiders were whirling their horses and galloping away, putting as much distance as they could between themselves and the trio of lawmen. The two wounded men, who were badly hurt from the looks of it, managed to trail along behind the others.

Seth lowered his rifle and said excitedly, "We really put the run on 'em! Are we going after them, Cody?"

Pointing, Cody said, "Looks like you boys are going to have another job."

The three surviving horses of the team that had been pulling the wagon had finally broken free, and now the animals were galloping wildly down the road. Cody went on, "You two go round up those critters while I check on the folks at the wagon. I don't think the owlhoots'll double back and cause any more trouble, but keep your eyes open just in case."

Seth and Alan nodded, sliding their rifles back into their sheaths, then rode off after the stampeding draft horses.

Drawing nearer to the wagon, Cody saw four people emerging from the shelter of the overturned vehicle. As he had already determined, one of them was a woman, and the sun was shining on her light brown hair. He brought his horse to a halt and studied the three men with her. They were a mixed group. One was elderly, one was young, and one was in between. The older man and the youngster were dressed like easterners, while the middle-aged individual was obviously a frontiersman. He was the one who raised a hand in greeting to Cody.

"Howdy, mister," the man said. "You and your pards

sure saved our bacon. Mighty lucky you showed up when you did."

"Anybody hurt here?" Cody asked.

"Miraculously, none of us seem to have been injured, even in the calamitous overturning of our wagon," the older of the two easterners replied. "The only fatality was that poor horse, and I think it was pure bad luck that he was hit. For all their savagery, those brigands did not appear to be very good shots."

Cody nodded. "They'd've closed in when they got tired of their little game. What are you folks doing out here by yourselves, anyway?"

"We are on our way to Del Rio, sir. I'm Dr. Henry Sedgewick. This is my niece, Miss Jacqueline Martin; my assistant, Royce Emerson; and our guide, Mr. Tom Harvey. And you are? . . ."

"Name's Cody." He reached down to clasp the hand that Henry Sedgewick extended to him. "Front handle whittled down to Sam. But most folks just use the last one. Pleased to meet you, Doctor."

"And we're quite pleased to make your acquaintance as well, Mr. Cody, I assure you." He nodded at the silver star on a silver circle pinned to Cody's vest and asked, "I take it you and your friends are lawmen."

"That's right. We're riding for the Rangers."

Cody kept an eye on the man called Tom Harvey as he spoke, and he thought he saw a flicker of reaction in the guide's eyes. He'd heard of Harvey, and not everything he'd heard was good. Not even most of it, in fact.

Looking over the group, Cody felt a tingle of misgiving. This bunch was just trouble waiting to happen, and he was a little surprised it had been this long in coming.

Dr. Henry Sedgewick was tall and slender and stoop-shouldered, but maybe not quite as old as Cody had first taken him to be. He wore thick spectacles, and his thinning hair was more gray than brown. His outfit of frock coat, dark trousers, white shirt, and carefully knotted necktie might have made him look like some sort of dandy, had it not been so dusty and threadbare.

The young man beside him, Royce Emerson, wasn't wearing a coat or tie, but he, too, had on a white shirt and dress pants. He was stocky and moonfaced with dark curly hair, and there was a smudge of gunpowder across his cheek. He had been firing a single-shot rifle toward the outlaws without much success when Cody and the others had arrived. Cody figured he was in his early twenties. Probably had never been west of the Mississippi until now, either.

Sedgewick's niece, Jacqueline Martin, looked to be slightly younger than Emerson. She was pretty, with long brown hair and green eyes which looked up intently at Cody, and her body in a white blouse and ankle-length brown skirt was smoothly and gracefully curved. Her gaze flashed with intelligence. A young woman like her would be quite a prize, Cody sensed, here in the West or anywhere else.

If the three easterners seemed a bit out of place to Cody, then Tom Harvey was all too familiar. Even though Cody had never run into him before, he'd seen the same type many times. Harvey's denim pants were worn, his buckskin shirt was faded, and the battered Stetson had been shoved to the back of his head to reveal a tangled thatch of lank, dark blond hair. A moustache of the same shade hung over his wide mouth. He wore a holstered Colt and was carrying a Spencer carbine. Even at the range the bandits had been staying during their attack, Harvey should have been able to hit something with a weapon like that, Cody thought. The man was somewhere in his forties, the Ranger guessed, and had been out here on the Texas frontier for a long time. He wouldn't have survived as long as he had if he hadn't been a good shot.

It was too soon to suspect Harvey of anything underhanded. Cody didn't like jumping to conclusions, and he had just met these people. But he filed his doubts about Harvey anyway, thinking that it might be a good idea to discreetly inform Sedgewick about some of the rumors concerning the man he had selected as a guide.

Royce Emerson spoke up, pointing down the road and saying, "Look! Your colleagues caught our horses, Mr. Cody."

Cody shifted in his saddle and glanced over his shoulder. Sure enough, Alan and Seth were herding the runaway animals back toward the scene of the wreck.

"I must check on my equipment," Sedgewick muttered, more to himself than anyone else. He hurried toward the rear of the wagon.

Cody overheard the doctor's statement and swung down from his saddle. He let the dun's reins dangle, knowing the horse wouldn't go anywhere. Curious about what might be in the wagon, he fell in step beside Sedgewick. "Would that be medical equipment you're referring to, Doctor?" he asked. "This part of the country could always use another sawbones, if you're planning on settling around here."

"Sawbones?" Sedgewick echoed, confusion in his voice. "Oh, you mean a physician! No, no, Mr. Cody, I'm afraid you misunderstand. I hold a doctorate in history, not medicine. I'm a professor at Norwood University in Pennsylvania."

Cody grinned sheepishly. "Oh. Reckon you're the first professor I've ever run into." He paused, then added, "If you don't mind my asking, why're you in these parts, Doctor?"

But, apparently distracted, Sedgewick didn't answer. He had stooped to peer under the rear of the wagon's canvas cover and was gazing intently inside. It was a large vehicle, almost as big as a Conestoga, but rather than the white canvas that usually covered the top of such prairie schooners, the fabric on this wagon had been dyed black, so that it reminded Cody somewhat of a hearse. Also, it was squared off at the top, like an army ambulance wagon, rather than rounded. All in all, it made quite a distinctive impression.

"What excellent luck!" Sedgewick exclaimed, throwing back the canvas so that Cody could also bend over slightly and see into the interior of the wagon. "None of the chemical bottles were broken in the accident. I imagine they'd be quite difficult to replace out here. There's not a photographic supply house in Del Rio, is there?"

With a frown, Cody studied the array of equipment inside the wagon. Much of it had been overturned or had tumbled off storage shelves during the pursuit by the outlaws and the resulting crash, but he recognized a bulky, boxlike camera on a folding tripod, thick glass bottles containing noxious-looking liquids, metal trays and containers, and padded wooden boxes that held photographic plates. The Ranger glanced over at Sedgewick and declared, "You're a picture taker!"

"Indeed. To be precise, I am a student of the art of photography. You must be familiar with it, Mr. Cody."

"Yeah. Fella who comes through Del Rio every now and then, he makes daguerreotypes for anybody who's interested and who's got the price. I never had the time to sit still long enough for one of 'em."

Sedgewick waved a hand. "Daguerreotypes! Fine for their day, I suppose, but I much prefer the collodion process. It was developed in England by a man named Archer a few years ago. Less time is required for exposure and developing, and I'm of the opinion that it produces a better image, as well."

Royce Emerson had wandered over and was studying the jumble of equipment and apparatus inside the wagon while his employer spoke. As the professor concluded, Royce glanced up and added, "Dr. Sedgewick can take your picture in a matter of minutes, Mr. Cody, instead of making you sit still for a half hour or more while the plate is being exposed. And there are new advances coming along every day."

Sedgewick smiled. "Of all my students, Royce was the one who most shared my enthusiasm for this exciting new art. That's why I hired him to accompany us."

Cody thumbed his Stetson to the back of his head. "Well, I don't know much about this photography business, but I know you've got a mess in there. Be easier to clean up once we've got the wagon righted."

Tom Harvey asked, "How're you goin' to do that? Wagon's mighty heavy."

Cody looked around. "There're enough of us men here to be able to lift it back up onto its wheels, I'd say."

The guide didn't look overly pleased at the prospect of such manual labor, but he only grunted and didn't protest. Seth and Alan rode up, driving the draft horses in front of them.

"Best hobble those horses so they don't run off again," Cody told the younger Rangers. "Then you can give us a hand with the wagon."

The three Rangers turned toward the vehicle. Sedgewick and Royce emerged from the back of it, each of them with their arms full of some of the scattered equipment from inside. The professor said, "I thought it might be a good idea to remove the plates and the chemicals before we attempt to set the wagon upright. These items have already been bounced around more than they should be."

"That's fine," Cody said. "You just tell us when you're ready."

The professor and his assistant made two more trips

into the wagon, each time storing the things they had removed to one side of the road. Finally Sedgewick brushed his slender hands together and announced, "That should do it. Gentlemen?"

As the Rangers stepped up to the wagon, Cody waved Sedgewick back. "Better let us handle this, Doctor. I don't think there's room for all six of us up here. Come on, Harvey."

Tom Harvey grimaced and stepped forward. Sedgewick hesitated and asked Cody, "Are you sure? . . ."

"You just step back there with your niece, sir," Cody told him. "Might ought to keep an eye on those horses to make sure they don't bolt again."

Sedgewick nodded. "Of course. Good idea."

That let the professor feel a little more useful, Cody thought. Actually, he doubted that Sedgewick's strength was sufficient to help any. It was better that he stay out of the way.

Cody positioned himself at the center of the wagon, facing the top of it, with Seth and Alan flanking him. Tom Harvey and Royce Emerson stood at the front and rear of the vehicle, respectively, and reached around to find suitable handholds. The three Rangers bent over and grasped the frame that held the canvas covering. Cody said, "Once we get it started up, get under it as quick as you can so this frame doesn't have to bear the weight for too long."

Seth and Alan mumbled their acknowledgment, while Emerson said, "Yes, sir!" Saying nothing, Harvey just spat on the ground and got a better grip on the wagon.

"Everybody ready? . . . Heave!"

At Cody's command the five men put their backs into the task. With grunts of effort they strained against the heavy wagon, and it slowly began to lift. When the side it had landed on had been raised several feet off the ground, Cody snapped, "Get the bed!" Seth and Alan released their grips on the frame and dropped their hands to the bottom of the wagon bed, which was now within reach. Flushed with the strain, they kept lifting until the weight of the wagon suddenly shifted and it dropped down onto all four wheels. The men stepped back, huffing and blowing.

"Damned hot for work like that," Tom Harvey complained, taking off his hat and wiping sweat from his forehead.

"Hotter for walking," Cody pointed out. "Seth, cut that dead horse loose and take a look at the broken harness. We'll need to rig something to hitch up the rest of the team."

While Seth was attending to that, Cody stooped down and looked over the framework and suspension of the wagon, now that it was upright and the weight of it was resting on the wheels again. After a few moments he straightened and nodded in satisfaction.

"Reckon it'll travel all right," he announced. "Wheels don't look damaged, and the axles aren't cracked." He turned to Sedgewick. "I think you should be able to make Del Rio without any more trouble, Doctor."

"Thanks to you and your friends, Mr. Cody." The professor gestured toward the equipment stacked beside the road. "I've been examining my gear, and other than a few glass plates being broken, there's no damage. I'd say we came out of that encounter with the bandits remarkably well."

Especially considering that they could've all been killed, Cody thought, but he didn't point that out. He said, "Losing that horse'll slow you down a little, but you can pick up another one when you get to town."

"Excellent. I'm eager to continue with the expedition."

"Expedition?" Cody repeated.

"My photographic expedition," Sedgewick said. "I'm sorry. I never did answer your question did I, Mr.

Cody? That's our purpose in coming out here this summer. I've been saving money for years to finance this journey across the Southwest. I intend to combine my two interests—history and photography—and make a photographic record of the historic places of this region."

Alan had been standing there, listening, and now he snorted. "You won't find much history around here, Doc. Just a bunch of sagebrush and mesquite and some folks trying to scratch out a living while they fight off owlhoots and redskins. Nobody'd ever be interested in that."

Sedgewick smiled. "I think you'll be proven wrong, my young friend . . . by history itself."

"Well, I reckon we'll see," Alan said. "If we live long enough, that is."

Seth came over and told Cody, "I can mend that harness. It'll take a little while, but we ought to be ready to go in half an hour or so."

The older Ranger nodded. "Then Miss Martin ought to go over to that tree and get in the shade until then," he suggested. "No need in you standing out in the sun, ma'am."

"Thank you, Mr. Cody," the young woman said with a smile. "I'll do that, if you don't need my help for anything."

"Not right now."

Jacqueline smiled at him again and went over to stand beside a rather scrubby live oak that nonetheless provided some welcome relief from the hot sunshine. Cody grinned to himself as he eyed his companions. Both of them looked as if they could kick themselves for not thinking to suggest the same thing to the pretty young woman.

"Get started on the harness," Cody said to Seth. "Alan and I'll help Dr. Sedgewick and Mr. Emerson get their things back into the wagon."

As they placed the equipment in the vehicle once

more, Sedgewick asked, "What do you think of my plans, Mr. Cody? Do you believe such a photographic expedition is worthwhile?"

The big Ranger hesitated for a moment, then said, "Reckon it can be. I've heard tell that that fella Matthew Brady took a lot of pictures during the War between the States. Folks'll probably be looking at those for a long time to come, trying to see how it was and figure out why it all happened."

"Exactly!" Sedgewick's voice quivered slightly with the fervor of his emotions. "Brady is a hero of sorts to me. I'd like to do for the Southwest and all its various struggles what he did for the Civil War."

"Then you've got a heap of work in front of you, Doctor," Cody said dryly, "because folks've been fighting amongst themselves down here for a long, long time."

When the wagon had been loaded, Alan wandered over to help Seth with the harness-mending job, while Henry Sedgewick and Royce Emerson straightened up things in the wagon. Cody went over to his dun and unlooped the strap of his canteen from the saddle horn. He had just taken a drink when Tom Harvey sidled up to him. Without preamble, the guide said, "Look, Cody, we appreciate you and your pards pitchin' in like you did, but if you're thinkin' about goin' on into Del Rio with us . . . well, there ain't no need."

As a matter of fact, Cody hadn't been thinking about that. It just seemed like a natural conclusion, one that didn't require any thought. He and his companions were heading for Del Rio anyway. Of course they'd ride along with the wagon, just in case the outlaws decided to try hijacking it again.

Cody waited until he had deliberately recapped the canteen and hung it from the saddle again before he replied to Harvey's statement. Then he said simply,

"We're all going the same direction. Might as well ride together."

The guide's jaw tightened, and Cody thought he saw the momentary glitter of something in Harvey's eyes. But then the man shrugged and said, "Sure, whatever you want, Ranger. Just figured if you had somethin' else to do—"

"*Nada*," Cody cut in. "*Nada* damn thing."

Harvey didn't laugh or even smile at the old border joke. He just grunted—which seemed to be his favored response—and turned away.

More than ever Cody suspected that he and Seth and Alan would be doing the right thing by accompanying the wagon on into Del Rio. And he was going to keep an eye on Tom Harvey the whole way.